Fallen Gods

By: Quinn W. Buckland

Fallen Gods

© April 17 2019 Quinn W Buckland

All rights reserved.

Cover by: Myself

Author Photo by: Buckland Imagery

ISBN: 978-1-9993961-1-4

First Edition

This book is dedicated to you.

As a reader of my books, you have become one of the most important people of my world.

You help me continue as an author.

You help me legitimize my craft

This one is for everyone who reads my books.

Thank you.

Also by Quinn W Buckland

The Engine What Runs the World

Warning

This book contains ideas and opinions that may be upsetting to some readers, especially those of the religious variety.

Many of the opinions within this book are not shared by the author, but are used to advance the story. After all, this takes place in a fictional universe.

Reader's discretion has been advised.

Chapter 1

"Is that thing on?" she asked.

Sam looked at the goddess standing by the large plate glass window. She was tall, with long dirty blonde hair falling past her shoulders in loose curls. The reflection of the streetlights off the window gave her jacket a blood-red hue.

Near the table he'd set up, his video camera stood on a tall tripod, ready to record every word she said and every movement she made. The boom microphone hung over the table out of the shot, but close enough that he'd be able to hear every word.

"Yeah, it's on. Proceed when you're ready," he told her.

The goddess walked toward the table in the nearly empty room. Her movements were fluid; she glided toward him as if she were walking on air. As she sat, Sam could see a slight smirk cross her lips.

"How would you like me to start?" she asked, her voice calmer than he'd expected.

Sam swallowed the lump building in his throat; he still couldn't believe he was sitting with someone of divine origin. Had she not shown him what she was capable of, he never would have believed her.

"Introduce yourself. After that you can start your story. How do you feel about questions as we go?"

"If you look lost or confused, I will let you ask your questions, but I would prefer if you remained silent during the story."

Sam nodded. "Very well, when you're ready."

The goddess cleared her throat, her smirk fading into an emotionless visage.

"My name is Athena. I am the daughter of Zeus, the goddess of wisdom, warfare, divine intelligence, architecture and crafts. I am the patron Goddess of Athens; my symbols include the owl, snake and olive tree. My home, long ago, was atop Mount Olympus, although I have not lived there for well over a thousand years.

"I have several brothers and sisters, many of whom I have recently seen die at the hands of our enemy. You see, the old gods are dying. It's not because of age, or lack of worship. Such things are inconsequential to our lifespans . . . for the most part, anyway. There's a war going on, and we're losing. I've already lost so many of my friends, my brothers, my sisters."

Sam thought she was feeding him the opportunity to say, "I didn't think gods could die. You guys are immortal. Nothing should be able to actually kill you."

Athena frowned. She didn't appear angry, just annoyed at the thought. He realized she hadn't baited him to ask the question, as he'd assumed.

"Gods can die. Take what happened between Loki and Baldr. Loki created a spear from the one lifeform who did not swear to never harm Baldr, mistletoe. It was a weapon created by a god for the intention to kill a god."

Athena's face darkened as she leaned in.

"Every god has a weapon. Thor has his hammer Mjolnir, Set has a spear, Poseidon has his trident and the list goes on. Each weapon is a device of great power for both creation and destruction. Those are the weapons able to kill gods, but only if that is the sole intention of the blow.

"The death of a god is a big deal. It's not like when a mortal dies. When you die, your soul is expelled from your body and sent to the underworld to be judged. You are then punished or rewarded based on your actions during life. When gods die, they also go to the underworld for a short amount of time. If they are not resurrected in time, they fade from existence."

"How long do gods have before they die for good?"

Athena shrugged. "It's hard to say. It depends on the god."

Sam smiled slightly, in an attempt to improve the mood in the room. However, his nerves made his smile one of fear than lightheartedness.

"So, all the stories in mythology are real?"

Athena chuckled. Her genuine smile was a pleasant sight. "Not quite, some stories are just that, stories created by people."

Sam gave her an odd look. "Which ones aren't real? That would be something my listeners would love to hear about."

Athena shook her head. "What's only story and what was once real is irrelevant. It has little to do with my story, though there may be some bits that open your eyes considerably. I will ask that you sit and listen, remaining silent. I will answer any metaphysical questions that you have at the end if I have time. I do apologise though; I am not a skilled storyteller as Calliope used to be."

"Please," Sam said, "just one question before you start."

Athena groaned with impatience. "Make it quick."

"Why are you talking like that?"

"Like what?"

"You know exactly what I'm talking about," Sam said. "You can cut that out. If you've been around for a thousand years, you can at least talk normally. You sound like you've just walked out of a goddamn Renaissance fair."

Athena took in a deep breath and exhaled loudly. Sam could see she was deciding on the words she'd use.

"Okay, fine," she finally said. "Fair enough. Now, can I get to my story?"

She glared at Sam until he nodded in agreement. Athena closed her eyes and waved her head from side to side. Soon she opened her eyes and spoke.

"There was a time when populations stopped believing in our existence. Maybe we were not doing enough for them to keep faith, or science was giving them the answers they previously didn't have. The why is not important, at least not anymore. The past is the past; it's the repercussions of the lack of faith, that's what is important.

"You see, deities are complex beings. Our existence doesn't come from being born and growing. We come from the imaginations of others. We form and grow based on the stories shared and the number of believers we have. As such, our power is dependent on our worshipers. Have a civilization or two worshiping you, and you'll have power beyond human comprehension. If you've only got a small city or a settlement worshiping you, well, you can figure that one out well enough.

"Yahweh, the little shit that he was, had been around for a while, but nobody really paid any attention to him. He was a Middle Eastern god; we believed those of us in the west were fine, especially since faiths didn't really wander too far. There wasn't any possible way for his followers to take over."

Athena paused and scratched the back of her head. "I'm sad to say, we were unfortunately wrong. We Olympians felt the effects first, after his followers set themselves up in Rome. Anyway, once Christianity began to form and became something important, people flocked toward it. They abandoned their faith for the deity Yahweh, gaining him power way faster than any of us could have possibly imagined.

"Just before the first crusade, Zeus received a letter from Yahweh stating he wanted to strike a deal with us. After all, he didn't want to go to war if he could avoid it. If he had, we'd probably have been decimated. I made sure to tell Zeus as much, we only had a few actual good fighters and no monsters to help us. Yahweh, on the other hand, had an army of angels. Beings he could create from almost nothing and let loose as disposable warriors.

"Unbeknownst to almost everyone on Olympus, I'd actually

been watching the wars Yahweh waged with the Egyptians. I watched in awe and horror as their once great pantheon was reduced to a fraction of what it used to be.

"Anyway, Yahweh's letter said he was going to send three of his archangels to each of the pantheons he wanted gone. That was us, the Egyptians and the recently-born Asgardians. I should note that Yahweh didn't want to kill us. He still had respect for us and our history, but he saw a new age coming, one we all had overlooked. We agreed to meet with the angels and come to an agreement. But we didn't exactly trust Yahweh or his angels. There was no telling what Yahweh wanted of us, or what we'd lose.

"So, we made a plan of our own, one to make sure we gods were not completely declawed."

Athena sat on her throne anxiously, waiting for the archangels to arrive. Seven of the twelve thrones in the circle chamber were occupied by gods: Zeus, Poseidon, Hades, Dionysus, Ares and Hera joined her.

Athena could feel the tension growing as every second passed. Ares began to emit a low, angry chest growl. It was he who took the news the hardest. He couldn't believe a pantheon as powerful as theirs was willing to surrender and kowtow to a deity barely old enough to know the spin of the world. Athena rolled her eyes as her brother fought a tantrum.

Zeus had chosen each deity for specific reasons. Poseidon and Hades were his brothers. In the beginning, when they'd first achieved deity status, the brothers had agreed to split their realms to rule individually. It was their right to be in any meeting that could shape the whole of the pantheon. On top of that, Zeus knew he would appreciate Hades' level-headed honesty and Poseidon's brash ideas.

Athena herself was there for her wisdom and ability to know which course of action would be best. Ares was present as a protective measure, just in case they were betrayed. Hera was there due to her marriage to Zeus; and Dionysus was there to keep everyone calm.

A small orange flash in the sky signalled the arrival. The descending angels had a beauty Athena didn't know existed. The centre angel had a visage of pure androgyny, appearing neither male nor female; its long brown hair flowed behind it weightlessly.

The angel on the left showcased heavy muscular arms, a strong jaw and all that pertained to masculinity, his red hair flowing down to his shoulders. Not a hair moved as he flew.

The final angel appeared female with soft features and a delicate build, her blonde hair flowing streaming wildly. Athena doubted that angels had any real gender, regardless of how they appeared. She allowed herself to be enamoured and taken in by their beauty.

Zeus stood as the centre angel walked forward. "Welcome to Olympus."

The archangel bowed. "Great and honourable Zeus, it pleases us and our father that you are willing to meet."

Zeus smiled as he walked towards the archangels.

"As king of Olympus, allow me to say your presence honours us. As per our agreement, I have brought six of my pantheon to be my council."

The angels looked at each of them. The red-haired angel looked disgusted with what he saw, while the blonde appeared genuinely pleased to meet them.

"My name is Michael," said the brown-haired angel. "The angel to my left is Raphael and to my right is Gabriel."

Raphael scrunched his nose at them. "Before we begin, does anyone have any questions or anything they would like to say?"

Ares grinned. "Yeah, I've got something I'd like to say. Die!"

Before anyone had a chance to react, Ares had bolted from his seat and charged toward the angels with his sword drawn. Zeus pointed at Ares, firing a bolt of lightning before the God of War's feet.

"Enough!" Zeus bellowed, the force of his voice shaking the ground beneath them.

Ares bowed his head.

"My apologies father, but I find it insulting to us and to you that Yahweh would send his lowly messengers instead of coming to us himself for something so important. I understand that this deal is important to our survival, but it doesn't excuse the insult, especially having to endure the rudeness of Raphael."

Zeus gave Ares a stern look. "Ares, you are going to sit down and keep quiet unless I say otherwise. Do you understand?"

Ares gritted his teeth. "I understand, father." He turned and sat down on his blood-red throne.

Michael bowed his head. "I apologise for my father's absence, but he is busy spreading his word into the hearts of all his children."

"You mean the mortals?" Dionysus asked.

Michael turned his head towards the God of Wine. "Dionysus, I don't understand why you refer to the humans as mere mortals. The term mortal can be insulting and could very well be why they are rejecting you. From what I've seen, you are a jealous bunch choosing to punish instead of guiding the way to enlightenment."

Hades laughed at the angel.

"Correct me if I'm mistaken, but from what I can see we both have a punish-and-reward system for the afterlife. You guys have Heaven and Hell while we have Elysium and Tartarus. When it comes down to it there's not any difference. The good get rewarded while the wicked get punished. Both systems create and manipulate humans to do our will, whether for their benefit or not. You can't deny it, Michael, and wipe that look off your face, Raphael. The only reason I'm agreeing to this farce is because I know nothing will change for the humans."

Gabriel smiled peacefully at Hades.

"You're right, Hades, we are the same. Perhaps my brothers and I did arrive here with pride, and for that we beg you to accept our most humble apologies. We could all take a few lessons in humility from you. You greatly care for the race of man, and you worry and wonder if under our rule things will become tyrannical, which I can assure you they will not. It is quite clear we are all biased in our own ways and believe our culture is what is best for our people. The purpose of this deal is to be sure you are comfortable with the change and you can leave knowing mankind will be in good hands."

Athena nodded in approval. She liked Gabriel; the angel gave her the impression of kindness and passion. Raphael, however, snorted. "If we are done with all these pointless comparisons, we should get the negotiations started."

Zeus returned to his throne and looked at the angels. "Please, be seated."

Michael bowed. "If it's all the same to you, we prefer to stand."

Zeus waved the comment away. "Very well, where shall we begin?"

"I think we should start with your acceptance of standing down as deities and taking on lives befitting humans. Naturally, you will maintain your immortality and memories of the years that go by. We will even allow you to keep a small percentage of your powers. However, you will no longer be able to call yourselves gods, nor will you be permitted to ever return to your pantheon."

"Why do we need to leave our homes?" Hera asked.

"It's not for us to say. All I can tell you is it's the only way our deal could be completed. If it helps, our negotiations today will be what we hand to the gods of Asgard and the Egyptians."

Ares leered at them; his heavy breathing through gritted teeth was the embodiment of pure rage. "So, you're telling me that we are the first that you've talked to?"

Michael nodded. "Yes, we had to start somewhere."

Ares slammed his fist onto the throne. "Bullshit!" he shouted.

The angels each took a step back. Athena reached her arm toward Ares to stop him from continuing.

"I believe what my over-tempered brother is trying to say is that he doesn't believe that you are being completely honest with us. There must be an actual reason that you chose to speak with us first, beyond having to start somewhere."

This time it was only Gabriel and Raphael that looked nervous.

Michael had regained his composure.

"Yes, there is a reason we chose you to be first. The Asgardians are a warrior race. If we came to them first, we would be forced to go to war with them and run the risk of killing them all, taking heavy casualties in the process. The Egyptians are a proud race and have proven to be hostile in the past. Our war with them was heavily taxing on both sides. You Greeks are warriors, but you are also scholars, artists and philosophers. It was believed that your pantheon would be more receptive to negotiations and a peaceful resolution."

Zeus looked around his council. Athena and Hera were the first to nod their heads. Hades and Poseidon were next. Dionysus nodded his as well. Ares looked at the others as if they had betrayed him. Soon, however, he growled in anger before nodding his head.

Zeus looked towards the three angels. "We have agreed unanimously to do things peacefully."

Michael held out his hands with his palms up. A small flash of light began to shine from his palms. From the ground, a table and three stools rose from the granite floor.

"For this, we will sit. As we discussed before, you will have to leave Olympus and live among the humans. We will also require you to relinquish your godly weapons."

"Out of the question!" Ares and Poseidon roared together. "We will never hand over our weapons!" Ares bellowed.

Michael cocked his head, amused.

"What use would you have for them? If you needed to, you could easily kill a human with a normal weapon, or a rock, or with your bare hands. You have no need for them."

"How would you have us protect ourselves from the other gods?" Dionysus retorted. "There are more pantheons than just you, the Asgardians, the Egyptians and us. Some of them are more than a little hostile towards other deities. Not to mention that there may be some fighting between us and the other gods on the mortal plane."

Gabriel gave Dionysus a kind smile. "My dear Dionysus, you won't need to worry about that. You will be in the human world;

gods won't even look at you twice. Plus, the other gods that will be down there with you will be no more powerful than you will be. Also, with your immortality there is no way they could possibly harm you."

"Okay," Poseidon said, "but why us three? Of all the groups of divine beings, of all the pantheons, of all the gods the mortals hold so dearly, why us, the Asgardians and the Egyptians?"

Michael shrugged. "That's not for us to know. It is our father's will, and as such, we will see it carried out."

Athena could tell Zeus was caught between a rock and a hard place. He didn't want to appear weak to his pantheon while avoiding a war as well.

"All right," Zeus said, "we will agree to your terms if you agree to our terms."

"What are your requests?" Raphael huffed.

Zeus was the one to grin this time. "Allow us to take an aside and discuss our demands."

Michael's smile seemed to grow bigger. "Of course, take all the time you need. We'll be right here when you get back."

In a puff of smoke, the gods disappeared. Once the smoke dissipated, Raphael screamed in anger. "Can you believe the gall of those lesser beings? Demanding that they make their own requests alongside our own? We should have killed them right then and there."

"Which one do you think you could have taken?" Gabriel asked. "Think about it, how long have they been gods? Two thousand years? Three? More? They may be weaker than they've ever been, but I highly doubt that we could have taken down a single one of them. Their demigods have more celestial power than we do right now. They also have experience over us; they're well versed in the ways of war and combat. We wouldn't have stood a chance. The only ones we could have even had a smidgen of a chance fighting would have been Dionysus or Hera, and even those odds are tenuous at best. All the others would have us dead before we could even have a chance to swing a weapon. Remember, two of them are deities of war."

"Not the point," Raphael snorted.

"It is, though," said Gabriel "We are still very young. The Greek gods alone could take on pretty much our entire army — what's left of it, anyway. The only reason we're even winning against the Egyptians is due to our numbers. If they ever figure that out, we won't survive to see our father again.

"The only reason they are even agreeing with us instead of fighting us is because they're afraid. They are weaker than they have ever been, which is still stronger than we will ever be."

"Quiet, you two!" Michael snapped. "I'm getting a message from our father. Yes . . .of course . . . okay . . . but . . . okay, your will be done."

"What'd he say?" Gabriel asked.

Michael shook his head. He looked mildly dumbfounded.

"He said to agree to their terms. If they agree to all of our demands, we are to agree to any and all of theirs. Provided the demands are not beyond reason, we are to accept them."

Both angels bowed their heads in acceptance. They only had to wait a few more minutes before the gods returned. Michael gazed at them, his face returning to an unreadable blank.

"What did you decide on?"

Zeus spoke first. "Our first demand is for you to give us no less than a year to get our affairs in order."

"What affairs might those be?" Gabriel asked.

Zeus grinned. "You have your secrets, and we have ours."

"Very well," Michael said. "Granted."

"No mortal is to be punished for worshiping us, or any other deity. You preach freewill and this will be the proof," Hades said.

Raphael grinned. "Lucifer might take issue with that. Granted."

"We will agree to cast aside our weapons on the conditions that we put them in a chest of our own creation," Ares snarled. "You can put the chest wherever you choose, but the design is ours alone."

"Granted," Gabriel said.

Poseidon grinned as he spoke. "We will be anonymous to

mortals. None of them are to know who and what we are. Any example of our otherworldly powers, our agelessness and our spoken name will remain ignored or unseen by any human."

Michael broke his blank expression to laugh. "I just thought that went without saying. Granted."

Hera spoke next. "No deity is to be able to procreate. There must never be any progeny from any of us."

"Granted," Raphael said. "Nobody wants any half gods running around."

Dionysus was the next. "No deity is to be able to kill a mortal, accidental or otherwise."

"Granted," Gabriel replied.

Finally, Athena was able to get in her demand. "In the event that all six of the previous deals have been broken by either us gods or by any of you, we will reclaim our power, thus absorbing much of yours and we shall gain our equal right to rule the world as proper deities once again."

Gabriel and Raphael gave each other worried glances. Michael bowed his head.

"We agree to your terms."

The angels stood.

"I pray the day never comes for us to see you again," Gabriel said with a sigh. "I fear that would be a dreadful day and one we all would rue for the rest of existence."

"I agree," Athena said solemnly. "Fly steady."

Gabriel smiled at Athena and the three angels flew away.

"Hermes, come to me," Zeus said softly.

Before Zeus had a chance to breathe, the messenger of the gods floated before him.

"What can I do for you, Father?"

"I want you to fly to Egypt and Asgard. Tell Odin and Ra that I wish to speak to them about something of grave importance. Tell them it's about the impending deal with Yahweh they will eventually have to make. The angels haven't spoken to them yet and it may not be too late. Go, tell them. We leave Olympus in a year, forever."

Hermes nervously nodded his head and in an instant, he was gone. Hades approached his brother and asked, "What's your plan?"

Zeus gave his brother a grave look. "You remember Typhon?"

Fear passed over the face of the God of the Underworld. "No, you can't."

Zeus shook his head slightly. "We must. Typhon and Echidna must be reunited and procreate. They must be permitted to give birth to all the monsters our heroes killed so long ago. They will remain trapped in the mountain until such a day as we need them, and I'm sure we will need them."

Athena turned and grinned at the other gods standing in front of their respective thrones. Hephaestus, the smith of the gods, stood with his hammer ready. Aphrodite sat on her throne naked, with her legs crossed. The twins Artemis and Apollo stood silent. Demeter reclined with a sack of grain on her lap. Zeus addressed them all.

"We need to be quick to accomplish all we need to get done. In a year our powers will be gone, and our weapons will be disposed of. You all know of the archangels and what they came here for. That was obvious to us all before they even got here. They have agreed to give us exactly one year to get all our affairs in order before we have to leave. We have a lot to do and not a lot of time to do it in."

Athena regarded her father as the rest of the gods disappeared. She remained to see Zeus sit back in his throne and stare out to the vast beyond of Olympus. She heard Zeus mutter softly, under his breath, "Goodbye Olympus."

With those words, her heart broke.

Chapter 2

Sam opened his pack of cigarettes. He grabbed one and brought it to his lips. As he lit the cigarette, a gentle plume of smoke drifted upward. He leaned back in his chair and put his feet up on the table.

"I'm sorry, but I'm going to have to stop you," he said. "I have a few questions."

He could feel the annoyance Athena held deep within. "Very well," she said sternly.

He waited a couple of seconds to ask, just in case she was going to give him a sort of signal to ask. "All right. What happened at the meeting between Zeus, Odin and Ra?"

"I don't know," she said. "We were forbidden to even listen in on the conversation. When it comes down to the kings of the gods, you obey their every command without fail. You respect their commands or suffer their wrath."

"Fair enough," Sam said. "Now, about your own demands, can you explain the reasoning behind them?"

"Seriously? I actually have to spell it out?"

Sam raised his hands. "Whoa, take it easy. I understand, but some of my listeners might not. Make it easy for them."

Athena rolled her eyes. "Fine, I'll explain it. Hera demanded that no deity was permitted to sire progeny. This one is quite simple to figure out. If gods were to have kids, they would come out one of two ways. They would either be mortal, and we would have to suffer knowing that someday they would grow old and die; or they would be immortal and in a matter of a few centuries the whole planet would be populated with an abundance of immortals. It would only be a matter of time before your race died out because of it.

"Zeus demanded the year to prepare himself for the war that would inevitably arrive. He seemed to know we'd be betrayed in the end.

"Hades demanded that no mortal be sent to Hell for worshiping any gods other than Yahweh because it wouldn't be fair to them; he always believed that a person's reward or punishment was dependent on their actions, not their beliefs. Personally, I agree with that assessment. Besides, you are more likely to meet an atheist or an agnostic than to meet a pagan. The numbers are going up recently, but not by much. That said, it would not have been fair of him to punish those who follow a different deity and not the indecisive ones or the mortals who follow nothing."

Sam gave her a perplexed look. "Are you saying that atheists don't go to hell?"

Athena nodded. "Yeah, it's not what you believe that gets you to Elysium, it's your actions. Anyway, carrying on.

"Ares believed that if we the gods designed the crate, someday we would be able to access our weapons once again.

"Poseidon didn't want us to be noticed by the mortals. That request is also obvious as to its importance. If most people met us and recognised us for who we were, we would get nothing but people asking us to bless them and for help. We're technically no longer deities; therefore, we can't help.

"I don't really think I need to mention the reasoning behind my demand or Dionysus's demand. Those ones are pretty self-explanatory."

Sam sat at the table with a wide smile on his face. Everything he was getting was pure gold. This story would make him famous; he would be rich.

"I think that's all the questions I have for now. You can continue."

Athena nodded. "For over a thousand years we wandered the earth. The twenty-first century has been exceptionally generous to us. Zeus, Thor and I took on jobs at the Red City News station. Thor and Zeus were weathermen while I was an anchor."

"Oh yes, I know them!" Sam said in excitement. "Thomas Zapp and Zach Storm. They have the two-month forecast. And you, I thought I'd seen you before. You're Agatha Weis. I loved your report on the new wave of superhumans popping up in this city."

"I met a couple of them," Athena said, with a slight hint of pride.

"Really? Which ones?" Sam asked with the excitement of and eight-year-old boy.

"Just hold on and find out."

"That's so cool. What other gods would I know?"

"I'll get to that."

Athena passed by the news cameras. She moved around to the back side of the news table, passing her co-anchor Max Yarl. He gave her a slight smirk and said, "You sure this story is going to be alright? You know how judgmental the masses can be."

"Trust me; they are going to eat it up. Besides, I don't withhold the truth on a story that I feel they're going to want to hear."

He snickered softly in disgust. "Yeah I figured, and of course *you're* going to tell the story. You're the favourite anchor in Red City. As far as I'm concerned, you're just a whore looking to further her career."

Back in the day, Athena would have struck him for speaking to her in such a manner. This was not her world anymore, though; she couldn't smite him if she'd wanted to. She couldn't do anything about his comment but smile.

"Say what you want Max, at least I'm the one succeeding, not spiraling down a pit of snack cakes and whiskey."

The flabbergasted look on his face was reward enough. The

cameramen caught her attention as they began the countdown. Athena composed herself and waited for her cue.

"Good evening everyone, I'm Max Yarl."

"And I'm Agatha Weis."

Max began the night as he usually did with the small spectacle news. Something lighthearted and forgettable before he'd move on to the depressing stuff.

"Last night, strange lights were seen in the sky. Eyewitnesses claim there was a bright flash while seven small lights hovered in the air for several minutes before flying in different directions. NASA, Soc-Tech and Pantheon are looking into the origin of these lights to determine just what they could have been.

"Many believe the lights to be of extraterrestrial origins. Could there be aliens above us? If so, are we prepared to meet with them in peace? More on that after our program, when we will hear from Soc-Tech and NASA officials. Also, as a special guest, we will be bringing in Paul Johnson, the ghost leader from the Council of Supernatural Beings. All that and more, at ten."

Athena watched as the camera quickly panned over to her. She did her usual puff piece about a local dog centre being run by a man/dog creature. She'd known of his humanlike animal kind in the past, but ultimately never really thought much of it.

Max read another news item while Agatha prepared herself for her big story. The story that would get people talking for weeks.

"Back to you Agatha," Max said, eagerly awaiting to see what she had to say. She looked to him, nodded and peered back toward the camera.

"If you've been down the back alleys in the last couple of weeks, you may have noticed that you are able to walk in safety. The new superhero rumours sweeping over Red City have left the population in awe. However, the question of their existence has raised other questions. Where did they come from? Who are they? Will we be safe from them in a few years, as we are now? And perhaps most importantly, is there anyone who can legitimately prove the heroes exist? All I can do is give my own experience with them and provide my own proof of their legitimacy. If anyone wishes to go over my footage to see if it was doctored, I welcome you to do it."

The monitor turned on her pre-recorded video. She watched herself standing outside her apartment, microphone in hand.

"Two nights ago, I was alone at home when two masked criminals entered through my window. I didn't know it at first, but they were superpowered humans. The first one merely looked at me and froze me in my tracks; luckily, I was able to scream for help before he managed to use his power. I would have been robbed if not for the timely intervention from two heroes."

The image changed to her apartment footage as it played the events of the evening. The video was grainy and in black and white. Not the most compelling of evidence, as not much could be clearly seen. But it would convince the gullible and already-convinced. In all honesty, she really didn't have much to work with. She'd hoped her voice-over would help fill in the gaps.

The sound of Agatha's voice carried on over the footage.

"The male hero, as you can see, is able to move into and through the shadows. I managed to see him somehow controlling the shadows to create solid tendrils to whip and grab at the thieves. The woman that was with him was a skilled fighter. I can't say if she has powers; if so, they're well hidden. Once I was safe, they told me their names were The Night and The Velvet Rose. I managed to get a conversation in with The Velvet Rose as she made sure I was alright after the ordeal.

"Who they are and who they work for remains a mystery. But, I know after my rescue, they're all right by me. For Red City News, I'm Agatha Weis. "

The news camera moved back toward Agatha. "Back to you Max."

"Thank you, Agatha, I'm certain that we can all sleep a little more soundly knowing that humans with god-like powers are looking out for us. Now to our very own Thomas Zapp for his three-week forecast."

Thor came up on the monitor. He looked different than he did back in his Asgard days. His hair was short, and he was clean-shaven. He still had his muscular physique, but he moved with a more careful grace than when he was a blundering oaf.

She watched as he grinned and said, "Thank you Max. Today we can expect sunny skies and a high of twenty-three degrees Celsius. Tomorrow will be fifteen degrees Celsius with rain starting at about eleven in the morning and continuing for the rest of the day."

Loki peeked from behind the deep red curtain of the stage. The stadium held over a hundred thousand people, the largest crowd he had ever preformed before. He breathed a sigh to calm himself.

"I can do this. Not a problem at all."

"Scared?" asked a voice behind him.

Loki turned to see his manager. He was a short balding man with a greasy smile. Anyone who had half a brain wouldn't have gone anywhere near "Ol' Buzz McLachlan." Loki, however, saw that it wasn't because he was dishonest; in fact, Buzz was one of the most honest and hard-working men he had even known. Buzz just had a habit of taking high-risk deals that failed to pay off most of the time. While representing, Loki, however, both managed to become quite wealthy.

Loki nodded. "Yeah, I'm pretty nervous. I'd be dumb to not be. This crowd could easily make or break my career."

Buzz slapped Loki on the shoulder.

"You'll do just fine m'boy. You're the great Lance Mist, the hottest newcomer to the comedy circuit. You'll be the best one to walk onto that stage tonight. Trust me; Ol' Buzz McLachlan knows talent when he sees it."

Loki smiled. "Thanks Buzz, I needed that."

Loki watched as the lights in the auditorium dimmed and the spotlights hit the stage. The voice over the megaphone began.

"Ladies and gentlemen! Prepare yourselves for the greatest night of comedy mankind has ever known! Give it up for your first comedian of the night: Lance Mist!"

Lance straightened his spine and walked into the lights. .

Everyone clapped and cheered as he approached centre stage.

"Good evening everyone!" Loki shouted into the mic. "It's great to be back in my home town, Red City, the only place in Alberta that actually needs to announce it's actually a city."

The crowd laughed. Loki took in a breath and began his best set ever.

Hera, Isis and Hathor rushed towards the maternity ward.

"We have a Miss Janet Pierson, age twenty-two, about to give birth," Isis said as she looked at the young woman's chart.

Over the intercom a voice spoke. "Doctor Lang to the OR. Doctor Lang to the OR."

"Shit," Isis murmured. "Looks like I'm not going to be joining you."

Hera smiled. "It's fine, we can handle this. It's not like we've never delivered a child before."

Isis grinned as she turned and sped in the other direction. Hera and Hathor continued down the hall.

"So," Hathor asked Hera, "are you going to The Gathering?"

"Yeah, it's been a long time since I've seen any of my children. Plus, it's a good chance to talk to my husband. He's always so busy at the news station and I'm always here. We don't see each other very often anymore. Do you see anyone from your pantheon?"

"Other than Isis? No, not really. Honestly, I don't even miss them. The only one I ever come close to missing is Kohnshu. We talk occasionally, but not very often."

"What's he been up to lately?"

"Last I heard he was teaching Grade Three, here in Red City."

Hera gave her friend an odd look. "That's a strange job for a moon god."

Hathor snorted in amusement. "He's the God of the Moon and Youth. It kind of makes sense when you think about it."

Hera laughed. "I guess so."

As they approached the doors to the maternity ward, the two goddesses prepared themselves to bring a life into the world.

***

Aphrodite sat in her dressing room clad in nothing but her underwear. She was surrounded by mirrors and makeup. As she applied her mascara, she heard a harsh knock on the door. She checked to see that she was not exposed anywhere and turned towards the door.

"Come on in!"

The door opened to reveal Freyja and Beyla, her ex-manager and her assistant. Freyja was dressed in a suit, while Beyla looked more business casual and carried a clipboard.

"I see you've made yourself comfortable," Freyja said in a tone akin to spitting acid.

"What can I do for you, Frances?" Aphrodite asked in an impatient tone. "I have a shoot in twenty minutes. I need to get myself ready."

"Yes, I can see that." Freyja said, an angry flush on her cheeks. Her voice shook with fury.

"Well, at least your powers of observation haven't failed you. Can you please make this quick? I have a job to do."

"How long have you been a model for?" she huffed. "Fifteen years? That's twice as long as most get in this industry."

Aphrodite smirked. "Just goes to show how good I am."

"Do you know how much longer you have in this industry? I can sure as hell tell you!"

"Is this about the whole me firing you thing?" Aphrodite asked, standing. "Look, you're good, the best in the industry. I just don't need you anymore. I can make it with my popularity. Besides, I wanted a younger agent; one that has a better finger on the pulse of fashion."

Aphrodite looked out her door and could see a couple of the other models peering at them from a distance. "Could you close the door so we're not broadcasting to the entire fucking place?"

Beyla nodded and closed the door. The moment the door was closed, Freyja and Aphrodite smiled at one another. Aphrodite threw herself at Freyja and gave her a hug.

"Hey Aphro," Freyja said with a chuckle as she hugged back.

"How are you Beyla?" Aphrodite asked enthusiastically.

"I'm fine," Beyla said in her usual impartial monotone, not once looking up from her notepad and clipboard.

"I really hope this works out like we had planned," Aphrodite said nervously.

"It will," said Freyja, smiling broadly "We should have more than enough time to fall out of the spotlight. It will look like Beyla and I couldn't find work after you fired us and like the incompetent agent you hired will do nothing more than permanently ruin your career. We should be good come The Gathering in six months."

Aphrodite nodded. "Yeah, some have begun to notice that I'm not aging. It's going to become problematic if I don't fall from the limelight soon. Though I do feel bad about the agent whose career we will be ruining in the process."

"She'll be fine."

"Ma'am, your next meeting is in an hour," Beyla chimed in. "I know we'll be incognito in a little while, but until then we need to maintain our human facades."

"Yes of course." Freyja said "It was great to see you, Aphrodite. I'll see you again at the gathering."

Freyja shot Aphrodite one final grin before changing her face to a sour scowl. She slammed the door open, nearly knocking it off the hinges. Once she and Beyla exited the room she slammed the door. Aphrodite jumped up and swung it open.

"Yeah? Fuck you too, you cunt!" she screamed to Freyja's back, knowing full well she'd be out of the game for a couple decades or more.

The body on the stainless-steel slab lay covered in a white sheet. A slight gust shifted the light fabric from the corpse's arm as Hades, Hel and Anubis walked into the autopsy room. Hades approached the head of the slab, while Anubis took the left and Hel took the right. They turned on the overhead light and uncovered the body.

Anubis reached into his pocket and pulled out an old tape recorder, one he'd used for nearly twenty years. He handed the device to Hades who nodded to the others and pressed the record button.

"Our victim, Adrian Laar, is a twenty-seven-year-old male; height is six feet and four inches. Weight two hundred pounds and physically fit. The doctors preforming the autopsy are doctor Hank Tartros and my two assistants, Doctor Aaron Jackal and Doctor Helen Heim."

Hades paused for a moment to take a breath.

"The victim suffered multiple stab wounds to his arms, legs, chest and throat. Doctor Heim, care to give your assessment?"

Hel looked over the body. "The killer seemingly knows human anatomy. The stab wounds are not in random places. The wounds on both arms severed the brachial arteries, the wounds on the legs severed the femoral arteries and the throat wounds severed both jugulars. The wounds in the chest appear to have cut into the right ventricle and the right atrium. There's also a wound that could have cut through the myocardium. I'll be able to get a better analysis once we've cut him open, though based on the placing I would say that is what we will be looking at. They're too precise to be random."

"Doctor Jackal, what were the names of the officers who found the body?"

Anubis looked through the paperwork. "Detectives Natalie Flite and Stephen Kerr."

Hades looked at Anubis to show that he understood just who exactly they were talking about. Nephthys and Seker. They were the precinct's two best detectives. They had the highest solve rate of any detectives in the country. They would be the poster children of the cop world if they were not also known to have the highest body count of any detectives as well. Many commissioners had scratched their heads trying to figure out how they were able to take down drug smugglers and arms dealers without a scratch.

Hades grabbed a scalpel. "Making the first incision now. Hopefully we will have a better idea on what happened after the autopsy."

Anubis and Hel stood beside him to assist him with whatever he would need.

Ares, Sekhmet and Odin walked silently through the dense jungle of the Amazon rainforest, the only sound coming from the swing of Ares's machete as he cut through the tangled brush. Their mission: to find and eliminate a group of drug runners.

In the military, they had become famous and earned numerous medals of honour. In more recent days, they had become mercenaries working for the good of their employer. To mercenaries and to anyone they had taken down, they were aptly known as The Gods of War. They were an unstoppable team that walked away from every mission unscathed while anyone else would have never been found again.

"How much farther do you think it is?" Sekhmet asked quietly.

"Too far," Odin grunted.

Ares brought his machete down on a branch.

"It's bad enough that we have to track down an enemy deep in the fucking Amazon, but having to cut through all this? This is fucking bullshit. We should be able to just shift ourselves to their location, but no, we have to keep up appearances. If someone just appears out of nowhere and kills damn near everyone, questions will get asked. Even if they are a bunch of drug runners."

Odin grunted again. "Bitching again, Ares?"

His machete cut through a vine. "Yes, I know; we are the best of the best. The aptly and ironically named Gods of War."

Sekhmet shrugged. "It's still funny."

Odin shushed the two of them. Ares sneered and continued cutting.

"What's wrong Ares? Mosquitos getting to you?"

Ares was silent as he cut through a branch bigger than the machete should have cut through.

"It's all these little shit jobs we keep getting. Sure, they pay well, but I need a challenge. Guerrilla warfare is getting really old."

"What would you consider a challenge?" Sekhmet asked.

Ares stopped cutting and turned to face them.

"Troy was a challenge. The Great War was a challenge; World War fucking Two was a challenge. Korea and Vietnam were sort of challenging, but more annoying than anything. These days? All we get are little skirmishes in comparison. War means nothing to anybody anymore. Do you know what I mean? War at one time used to mean something. Battles were fought for king and country, to expand an empire, to protect a persons' home. There were so many reasons. Now? People fight for oil or because they don't like communism."

Ares stopped, resting his machete on his hip. "All honour in war is gone. All glory of war is gone. Soldiers no longer fight to protect their beliefs and their gods. People fight because they are told to fight, or they want to kill people.

"Even how we fight has been changed. It used to be close, it used to be personal. When you took a man's life, you knew that he was fighting for his survival just like you were. We separated the men from the boys. Now we have children and civilians using guns. Shooting someone means nothing to anyone. When you can kill someone from a distance it takes away from the gravity of death. You become removed from the actions you've committed, from the life you've taken.

"And sure, bows fire from distance, but it took effort to shoot a bow. You had to know how to aim; you had to have strength to draw the string back. Guns, you point and shoot. Most of the time, you don't even have to aim, just spray and pray. War makes me sick these days."

Sekhmet nodded along with every point Ares made. "You're right. I've had the same thought. But hey, look on the bright side."

Ares turned and continued cutting the foliage of the jungle. "What fucking bright side?"

Sekhmet grinned. "The Gathering is on in six months."

Ares did what he could to hide his smile from the others. She was right, The Gathering was coming soon, and it would be a glorious occasion. The thought of it lifted his spirit a little as he continued chopping through the brush.

Three vehicles pulled into the hall's parking lot. One was a black stretch limousine. One was a bright green wreck of a car, and the last was a red motorbike. The door to the limo opened and Amun stepped out. He was dressed in a black business suit with black sunglasses.

Freyr dismounted from his motorcycle. He removed his helmet and walked toward the front door. Once they reached the door, they turned and looked at the green car. When the driver's side door opened, a plume of marijuana smoke drifted upwards. As Dionysus exited his car a half dozen beer cans fell out. He belched loudly and walked towards the Egyptian and Norse gods.

"How's it going?" Dionysus asked rhetorically, his grin only half hidden by a grizzled beard.

Amun shook his head. "You're the Olympians sent to help us organise this?"

"Well yeah," Dionysus said, still smiling cheerily. "You supplied the equipment. Freyr here is funding everything. You really didn't need much more. Except I'm here to gather our food, beverages and entertainment; you know, the important stuff. The Gathering happens only once every hundred years, for only six months. I need to be sure we have one hell of a coffer loaded."

Freyr sighed loudly. "Fine, whatever. Let's just do this."

The three gods opened the front door to the hall in the middle of the Alberta countryside and entered the building.

Chapter 3

Sam lit another cigarette. "Who are Seker and Nephthys? You mentioned they had a massive body count. How is that possible? I thought you couldn't kill anyone."

Athena pointed towards the pack of cigarette. "Mind if I grab one of those from you?"

Sam pushed the pack towards her. "Help yourself."

She pulled a cigarette from the pack and sniffed it to take in the aroma of the tobacco. She put the filter between her lips and carefully lit the end. As it caught, she inhaled deeply and let the smoke escape her lungs.

"Do you remember a kidnapper who went by the code name 'The Predator' from about a decade ago?"

Sam nodded. "Yeah, he would kidnap children, rape them, torture them and then kill them days later. Last I heard, he disappeared after his thirteenth victim."

"That's because he never got the opportunity to get a fourteenth. Seker and Nephthys found him. When they saw what had become of the latest child, they lost control. They somehow harnessed their deity powers and atomized him instantly.

"The two of them lived in fear for quite some time after that; they were waiting for some form of divine retribution. But, when nothing happened, they continued to kill killers, rapists and all those who they figured deserved it. There was never a body afterward though, they made sure of it."

Sam grinned at her as she continued to puff away.

"So that means you can technically break any of the rules you want without anything happening to you?"

"Not exactly," Athena said. "We've been breaking rules. Four of them so far have already been broken. The rest should be quite soon now, actually."

"Which ones?"

Athena gave him a nasty look. "Can I please just get on with the story? If we waste any more time, I may not be able to finish."

Sam felt a lump grow in his throat. "Am I in danger?"

"No, but I am. I'm being hunted right now and if they find me before I have a chance to finish, my plan will fail. Or, I guess her plan will fail."

"Please, continue with your story. I promise I won't interrupt again."

Athena gave him an appreciative look and continued her story.

Athena opened her eyes and gasped in shock, finding herself in the middle of a desert. She shielded her eyes from the sun and looked around. The dunes spanned as far as her eyes could see. Confusion sank in as she assumed herself to have been transported to a plane of existence covered in sand. She then looked down at her attire, and saw she was dressed in a loose white cotton dress and shirt.

She walked over several dunes before she began to sweat. Half a dozen dunes later, sweat began to sting her eyes. She stopped to tear a strip off the bottom of her dress and wrapped it around her head. Soon after, the sweating stopped —not a cause for alarm, but troubling nonetheless. She tried to speak but no sound came out. Her thoughts came not as decipherable words, but as emotions and abstract waves through her mind.

She topped the crest of a dune and could just make out an

object in the distance. She squinted, using her hands to shield from the glare of the sun, and her eyes began to focus. Over the waves of sand, she saw a lone door standing atop a nearby dune.

Acting on instinct, Athena began to run toward the door. Whatever it was, it wasn't normal. Experience and general knowledge about such phenomena indicated the door was a portal to wherever she needed to go. She was being tested, she thought, and she'd have to get to the door before it disappeared.

Athena looked behind herself to see a burgeoning sandstorm quickly gaining on her. She pushed herself harder to get to the door. Time was running fast, as was the storm. She had precious seconds to get where she needed to be, or she ran the risk of being trapped in the desert forever.

As she approached, she could see the green door had a mural of a desert engraved on it. She reached for the knob before looking back once again; the sandstorm was almost on top of her. She spun the knob and swung the door open, but nothing more than a whorl of greens and blues within blackness greeted her. There was only one option if she planned to survive; she had to go through the door and hope for the best.

Athena didn't bother to look back again before she leapt into the darkness. The door slammed behind her as she fell, her mouth and nose filling with a foul liquid before she fell into unconsciousness.

Athena opened her eyes warily, only to see nothing but blue stone. She picked herself up and looked down at her new attire. She was wearing a light blue tank-top and tan khaki shorts. *What the fuck is going on?* Athena thought. *Hey, I'm actually able to think here. At least something's changed for the better.*

She took a moment to look around the cavern, lit by a form of green luminous fungus growing from the walls. Small glowing spores floated downward, giving the floor an eerie hue. She looked around for the door to find, unsurprisingly, it was no longer there. Peering ahead, she saw a door to one side of the cave, but it presented a problem. It stood on the other side of a massive chasm.

Athena approached the chasm, gaping from wall to wall. How deep was it? She looked around and found two rocks. As she picked up the first rock, she realized that the whole time she had been in the cave she had not heard a single sound; not her feet on the ground, the wind or even the slow trickling of water. She looked at the first rock in her hand and shrugged before throwing the stone at the wall. The rock flew through the air and soundlessly struck the stony precipice. Well, Athena thought, disappointed, that makes throwing anything down the pit pointless.

Suddenly, a light from above shone in, brighter than the moss and illuminating a set of armour resembling what she'd worn in her days on Olympus. Alongside the armour, her spear and shield had been hung on hooks, ready for use.

She continued looking around for anything she could use to get across the pit. It wasn't impossible to jump across — the sort of jump where she'd have to take a running start and be prepared to reach out to grab the edge. Difficult, but possible.

She sucked in a soundless breath through her nose and stepped back to the wall at the back of the cave. She took off across the cavern. As she prepared to jump across, a force of energy pushed her back, landing her on her tailbone. Athena screamed silently and rubbed her wounded bottom. She looked back to her armour and nodded. Looks like I have to wear my armour to jump across. At least, I hope that's all I need to do.

She approached the rack holding her armour and placed her hand upon the bronze breastplate; the metal was cool to the touch. Memories filled her mind as she recalled all the battles she'd fought wearing it. She grabbed the breastplate and slung it over her shoulders and around her body. Placing the helm over her head, she bent forward to grab the spear. Under her armour she felt her clothes dissolve away. She tied her leather thong sandals in a crisscrossed pattern to her knee, then tied her leg armour overtop.

Power surged through Athena as she prepared once again to jump across the gorge. She readied her sandaled feet, gripped her spear with a death grip, and held her shield at the ready. In a flash, she moved across the cave, pushing herself with all her might. The armour weighed heavily on her body, but the rush of power gave her a level of confidence she didn't have before. She knew she could make it.

I'm not Athena. I'm not Agatha Weis. I am the Goddess of Wisdom! A fucking goddess! I will NOT be stopped by some hole in the ground!

She leapt, her powerful legs launching her through the air. As she flew, she watched the gorge get larger. Her emotions steeled; fear wasn't an option. She looked ahead toward the door, preparing to land on the hard, stony floor.

With a thud, Athena landed. *I made it,* she thought; but there was no time for self-congratulation. She continued her momentum, running toward the door, her prize, her desire, her coveted destination. She gripped the door handle and looked back. The gorge had closed, leaving nothing but an empty cavern. Her eyes narrowed as she opened the door and walked through. She hadn't considered what might lie ahead. Instead, she allowed her goddess self to take over.

Athena stepped through the dark haze into an open field of grass. The tall grass reached to her navel and smelled of dew. She looked down to evaluate her armour and saw that nothing had changed.

"Well," she said, her eyes fluttering as she realized she could speak.

She looked around the field; only three yards away stood the door. Athena tried raising her leg to find her feet were stuck in place. "For fuck's sake," she snarled.

Overhead, the sky darkened. She looked up to see a beam of light peeking through the clouds, shining directly on her. She watched as several objects filled the gap in the sky, flying down toward her. As they approached, she could see they were beings — heavily armoured angels, lances ready and speeding toward her.

She tried to move; she'd need to take a battle stance or retreat. There would be no other way she could survive the attack. Instead, her feet held her firmly in place. She counted a dozen angels nearing battle range, with several more flying in.

Athena's lips curled into a defiant snarl.

"This is how it is then," she said. "So be it. Come at me, you fuckers!"

Before the first angel descended on her, the force holding her down released its power. She jumped at the angel, striking it in the chest with her spear. The angel vanished in a burst of light. Athena released a war cry as she leaped at the next angel, catching it between the shoulder blades with the point. Launching herself away from the falling angel before it could burst into light, she pierced the next two easily.

The fifth and sixth angels were also easy targets, though more were coming. If they continued to come at such an impressive pace and number, she'd be overrun and unable to defend herself. She speared the next angel in her line of sight and vaulted toward the red door. The angels followed her, some getting in the way. Athena pointed her spear downward, catching an angel in the throat. She passed through it when it burst.

When she hit the ground, only one angel stood before her. It was the blonde feminine angel. Gabriel. She grinned at Athena, speaking without sound. She saw the other angels retreat at the sight of their master.

"What do you want?" Athena asked.

Gabriel shed her weapons and armour until she stood nude. She gave Athena a nod, her soft smile matching the intense gaze that never left her eyes. Athena removed her own armour and weapons until she wore as little as the archangel. The angel was either making a peace offering or wanted to fight naked. Athena prided herself on honour; she would not face an unarmed opponent armed.

Gabriel appeared as if she were preparing for a fight, but instead she grinned and nodded once again. She turned and gripped the door handle. She opened the door, allowing Athena to pass.

Athena placed two fingers to her head. "Thank you," she said graciously.

She took one final look at the archangel and walked through the door.

Athena woke with a start. She sat up in bed, breathing heavily. She wiped the sweat from her forehead and looked at her digital alarm, sitting on the bedside table by the wall. The clock flashed 4:33 in bright red.

"Fuck," she sighed.

She pushed the covers off and walked to the living room. Her mind went over all the happenings of her dream. With each memory, her stomach sank. She grabbed the pack of cigarettes from her coffee table and stepped outside. She lit the smoke and took a nice long drag.

Cigarettes had always been non-addictive to deities. Their physiology wouldn't allow substance dependence, despite the mind-altering effects being present. Athena, along with all the other gods she knew, took advantage of this whenever Earth living got to be too much.

Athena enjoyed her cigarettes; she found they calmed her when she needed something to take the edge off. She knew the calm had come from stepping outside and not from the smoke itself, but taking a break outdoors without a cigarette seemed strange to her.

She drew in a deep breath of the cool night air, twirling off the ash from her smoke on the concrete stoop. Thoughts raced through her head as she tried to understand what she'd seen. Another question occurred to her: had she been the only one to have the dream?

She pulled her cell from her pocket and dialed Apollo's number. If anyone could decipher her dream, it would be him. She inhaled again as the dial tone chimed in her ear. She could feel her hands begin to shake; her nerves were shot. The line clicked as Apollo picked up the line.

"Hello?"

"Apollo?" she asked nervously.

"Athena?" Apollo's voice rang with surprise and excitement. "What's up?"

"I just had a dream," she said, her voice quivering.

Silence on the other end seemed to last for many minutes. "You had a what?" Apollo asked, clearly not believing.

"A dream," Athena repeated. "One of the few things we're not supposed to have! I had one, and I don't know what it means."

"That's impossible," Apollo said after another pause. "I'll talk to Sif when she wakes. If you had a dream, and I do mean a legitimate dream, there's no way you'd be the only one."

"Yeah, I thought so too," she agreed.

"Is there anything else you need?"

"No, that's all I needed to say. It's possible I experienced something else. I don't know. But I'm certain it was a dream, it felt just like something Morpheus-"

"Please don't mention him," Apollo interrupted.

"Still not on speaking terms?"

"It's not that," Apollo said. "I just don't want his attention, and neither do you. If you really did have a dream, I'll be giving that little shit a call. You can be sure of that. It's just best if someone with experience deals with him and his . . .reality."

"Let me know," Athena said, putting her cigarette out in the empty coffee can she kept half filled with dirty water.

"I sure will," Apollo said, his voice returning back to his usual cheery self. "Oh, I've actually been meaning to call you. We should do lunch sometime. You, me and Sif."

"What's the occasion?"

She almost heard Apollo laugh. "Do I need a reason to see my sister? It's been a while and we should catch up."

"That would be nice. How does Sunday sound?"

"Sunday sounds great. I'll see you then."

She didn't say goodbye but hung up. She didn't feel any better than before, but her hands had stopped shaking. The fear that had burrowed itself into her had been dug out by Apollo's words while she sat on her step.

She considered another cigarette, only to decide she didn't want another and walked back into her house. She rubbed her eyes in exhaustion. Deities didn't need sleep, but once sleep had been chosen, it was wise to get the full eight hours. Athena crawled back into bed and was asleep after five minutes of exhausted consciousness. Athena slept the rest of the night dreamlessly.

The café was a pleasant little place, quaint and redolent with the scent of freshly ground coffee beans. She took a seat and waited for a server to come take her drink order. Couples sat at individual tables, enjoying each other's company as they sat and talked and ate. Single people sat with books in their hands or at laptops, baked treats and rich coffees beside them as they read or worked.

There wasn't much in the way of seating for families or groups. The environment and table sizes weren't conducive to larger gatherings. Athena enjoyed the café for the intimacy the small venue offered. It was a place for people to sit and talk and eat.

"What can I get you?" a petite blonde woman asked.

"Just a coffee for now," Athena said. "I'm waiting on two others. I believe we'll be eating."

The server smiled at her "One coffee and three menus. I'll be right back."

The service was another reason Athena enjoyed the café; the owner took great pride in advertising that he had the best service in the city. From what Athena had seen, he wasn't lying. All the servers were friendly and prompt. She wasn't exactly sure what the owner did to ensure every customer got the best service they required, though she had never once thought to question it. The best she could think of was an incentive program.

Athena watched as Apollo and Sif walked through the door. She waved them over as the server brought her coffee.

"What can I get you two?" she asked, placing the menus on the table.

"Mint tea," Sif said.

"Iced tea," Apollo replied as he sat.

The server's cheerful demeanor didn't change as she walked away to gather drinks. The deities started with greetings and basic small talk about work and home lives. It wasn't until food orders had been placed that they decided to get down to business and discuss the dreams.

"You were right," Apollo said. "I had a dream and Sif had one as well."

Athena raised an eyebrow. "So something's going on."

Apollo nodded. "I'm afraid so."

"What were your dreams?" Athena asked.

Sif looked at the table, unsure of what she wanted to say, "There were three parts to it. In the first part, I was in a grassy field and a tornado was coming for me. I didn't escape until I was forced to jump down a hole. The hole led to a small dungeon. I found a seriously archaic torture device and had to agree to electrocute myself to escape. After that . . ."

Athena could see the fear in Sif's eyes. While the first two parts hadn't brought any real change in her stoic demeanor, thinking of the last room seemed to terrify her.

"There were six versions of me, all wearing different expressions," Sif continued. "They were small, maybe up to my knee. They danced in unison to a song I couldn't hear. Then Apollo showed up and gathered them into his arms. He started throwing them at me, each one absorbed by my body. Then he lunged at me, pinned me down and said something I couldn't hear. Then I woke up."

"In my dream," Apollo said, "I was flying through the air until I was knocked out of the sky. When I landed, I was in some sort of circus tent. There was this big German Shepherd looking at me; its hackles were up, and it snarled. I stood and chose to pet it before the tent dissolved, everything went black after that, and I could feel myself falling. When I finally managed to land, I saw Sif and myself merge together. I didn't know what to do until I saw the same German Shepherd running toward us I attacked the dog and then I woke up."

"My dream wasn't anything like either of yours," Athena said.

She explained her dream to them in as much detail as she could. The way they'd described their dreams had been simple and to the point. She didn't need to know what they'd seen; Athena couldn't have deciphered them if she'd tried. She'd only asked to be polite. Apollo, on the other hand, had a gift for being able to determine what parts of a dream could or should be taken literally and what might be taken as metaphor.

Once Athena had finished, she could see Apollo doing his best to process everything she'd said. Eventually, he shrugged.

"I'm not really sure what I can tell you. The dreams don't make any sense. You sure it was the archangel that let you pass?"

Athena nodded. "After I agreed to not fight her. I really have no idea what to make of that."

"Well," Apollo said, "if I were to take my best guess —and be aware, this is off-the-cuff deciphering — he desert indicated you needed to do something quickly, or that something was going to happen soon. The second part sounds like a test of bravery. You couldn't jump without your armour because it would have been too easy. You'd have needed your armour to add weight to your body. Somehow, I also think your dream was saying you must be battle-ready. That last part though, that concerns me."

"What are you thinking?" Athena asked.

She peered over at Sif, who listened intently, but had decided the conversation didn't need her. She looked back to Apollo when he said, "It means a battle is coming. The angels may or may not be metaphors. I mean, for a very long time we've seen them as the deadliest opponents we could ever face; it makes sense we, or you in this case, would see them as a threat. Your feet being unable to move could indicate there's no retreat from the battle, especially since you were only released after you'd accepted the battle.

"In any case, you're going to go through the fight of your life, but you're going to find a peaceful approach with a general or whoever is running the conflict."

Apollo paused for a moment, taking a sip from his iced tea.

"But, like I said, that's just an off-the-cuff reading. I would literally have to talk to Morpheus about what's going on. And you can be sure; I'm going to be talking to him very soon."

"Think you can find him?" Sif asked.

"I don't think I have much of a choice. Morpheus is the sort who could, and certainly would, put messages in dreams, especially dreams for gods. He would have had to put in a lot of effort to give us dreams, and I want to get to the bottom of this sooner rather than later. If he was trying to warn us about something, he could have done a better job of it."

"I agree, but maybe he did what he could," Athena said. "If the threat is as great as you think, maybe he didn't have a lot of time."

Apollo leaned his head to the right and shrugged.

"That's totally possible. Just more reason for me to track him down and figure out what's going on."

The server returned with the food. Conversation abated while they ate. Topics became substantially more lighthearted afterward, turning to jobs and personal lives. Athena wasn't surprised at how pleasant the lunch with Apollo had been; he had always been one of her favourite siblings.

Once everyone finished their meals and paid, Apollo stood. "It was great seeing you," he said with a soft smile. "We'll have to do this more often."

Athena stood as well. "That would be great, Have a good drive back."

She hugged her brother and Sif before watching them leave. Athena stayed behind and ordered another coffee. She sighed, a look of contentment on her face. With Apollo on the case, she'd have answers sooner than later.

Chapter 4

From the outside, the building was not impressive — a single-storey hall in the middle of nowhere with peeling yellow paint and a dark brown sheet-metal roof surrounded by a large gravel parking lot. If anything, it looked like it should have been condemned and torn down decades ago.

The building had been a gift from Yahweh to the gods at the beginning of the twentieth century, a place they could safely hold their Gatherings in peace. The gift had been awarded for taking to Earth so kindly and continuing to be model members of society. Protective wards had been put in place to ensure the safety and sanctity of the hall. No mortal would ever be able to find it, no matter the circumstance.

Athena pulled into the gravel parking lot and found the last parking space. She let her motorbike's engine idle for a moment before letting it die, removed her helmet and hung it on the handle bar. She grinned as she stared at the dilapidated place. The weather hadn't been good to it, especially since they couldn't hire a caretaker to ensure a pristine exterior.

The gravel under her boots making a satisfying crunch with each step she took toward the building. She unzipped her leather jacket, revealing a plain white t-shirt to the world.

As Athena walked inside, the hall morphed from a dilapidated building to a pristine room nearly four times as large. Athena believed if any mortals were to experience the hall, their minds wouldn't be able to handle the size of the interior in comparison to the outside.

Ares, stationed in the main lobby, was watching the door. He was dressed in his battle armour. "Athena," he grunted, "you're nearly late, the last to arrive."

Athena shrugged. "At least I'm here."

Ares gave her an accepting nod as she hung her jacket on an over-stuffed coat rack and watched as her clothing changed. Her shirt and jeans morphed into a loose-fitting toga. From the top of her head sprouted a shining bronze helm with red plumage at the top, similar to what Ares wore.

She rolled her head along her shoulders with her eyes closed.

"It always feels so damn good to be back in my real clothes."

"Make sure to sign the guest book. It's a stupid idea, but Dionysus insisted upon it."

His final sentence had been grumbled under his breath. Athena clearly heard him, though she chose to ignore his negativity. She gleefully signed the book and proceeded to walk through the crowd of divine beings. She grinned and nodded as she gave her greetings to each Greek, Nordic and Egyptian she passed, each dressed in their native attire. The only difference was with the Egyptians; their animal forms had been denied as Yahweh believed them to be too dangerous. Instead, they wore the garb of their time.

In the far corner she spotted Apollo and made her way toward him, dipping and swerving through the clusters of deities engaged in conversation and drinking Olympian Ambrosia, Asgardian Mead or an Egyptian Heket.

She waved to Apollo as she caught his eye; he grinned in response. Once she was close enough to Apollo to talk to him, she dimmed the background noise around her.

Athena looked around, "Where's Sif?"

"I honestly couldn't tell you. She saw Bastet and took off. She's around through. How are you?"

"I'm alright," Athena said with a grin. "Happy to finally be at The Gathering. Did you ever figure out what was up with those dreams?"

Apollo shook his head.

"There are too many versions for me to go over. I'm still sure what I told you before is accurate. Still haven't a fucking clue as to what that last part is about, though."

"Did you talk to Morpheus about it?"

"I tried," Apollo said, "but he's missing. People are still having dreams, so I know he's alive somewhere, but I don't know where he went."

"Fuck."

"My sentiments exactly."

"So, what so we do now?"

"I don't think there's much we can do," Apollo said. "It's possible the dreams meant nothing, but since Morpheus is gone, I'm thinking there might be something else at work. He wouldn't give us all dreams for nothing. I think the best we can do is keep our eyes open and our heads on a swivel. It doesn't look like the dreams have affected anyone else. Nobody seems to be giving them much weight."

"They are, I can see it in their faces," Athena said, frowning "The smiles may be genuine, but I can see the fear in the corners of their eyes and mouths. But it's been five months since we had the dreams; maybe they're thinking nothing's going to happen."

"Maybe. I'm not so sure."

Athena put her hand on Apollo's shoulder. "We'll keep watch."

Apollo looked to his sister and grinned. "Damn straight."

The contents of Sif's stomach fell into the toilet. She'd felt the child growing inside her for nearly six hours, and already she was nauseated. She drew in a long, laboured breath as she hugged the porcelain bowl. The coolness of the toilet gave her arms goosebumps, and she wanted to get back to the party to celebrate another hundred years of life, but she couldn't seem to muster the energy to stand.

"You in here?" Bastet's voice called from the door.

"Yeah," Sif said, the feeling to retch persisting.

She spat into the toilet, attempting to get the taste of vomit out of her mouth.

"What's wrong?" Bastet asked, standing near the stall.

Sif exhaled sharply and stood. Her head swam, forcing her to close her eyes against the sudden vertigo.

"You wouldn't believe it if I told you."

"Girl," Bastet began, "I've known you almost a thousand years. We've been friends for most of it. There's nothing you can tell me that I wouldn't believe. So, what is it?"

Sif sighed and opened the door to the stall. "I'm pregnant," she said in a monotone.

Bastet's eyes grew wide "No fucking way. Hun, that's not something you joke about."

"Does it look like I'm joking?" Sif asked, her hand massaging her sore stomach. "I told you that you wouldn't believe me."

Bastet ran her fingers along her eyebrows.

"You're telling me to believe something that isn't supposed to happen."

"Like gods killing humans? Or cryptic dreams from nowhere?" Sif was starting to get annoyed. "Bastet, like it or not, strange shit is happening, and I am legitimately pregnant."

"Easy now," Bastet said. "You make a good point. All right, so you're pregnant. What do we do about this? Should we tell someone?"

Sif shook her head. "I have to tell Apollo first."

The look on Bastet's face would have made Sif burst into a fit of laughter had her stomach not been in pain.

"You haven't told him yet? How long have you known?"

Sif hung her head. "Since conception this morning. I felt the first cell divide and that was it. I haven't told him because I wanted him to enjoy The Gathering. The last thing I want is for him to be worried about me. Also, I don't want to be paraded around. You know

Apollo; he'd be showing me off. Yahweh would find out, terminate my pregnancy and that would be it."

"Would that really be the worst thing?"

"I know the treaty said no children," Sif said frowning, "but a pregnancy isn't supposed to happen. I got this baby for a reason, and I plan to see it through."

Sif could see Bastet thinking, and after a moment of silence she finally nodded and said, "All right, your secret is safe with me. But you'll have to tell Apollo sooner than later. You'll start showing by tonight. And you're guaranteed to have it in the next few days, so The Gathering is going to be interrupted anyway."

Deific pregnancies were fast affairs. Generally, they lasted no more than a couple of days, because the body of a goddess could give the child enough nutrients for a quick gestation period. Had Sif been given her full goddess powers, she'd have been able to slow the child's growth almost indefinitely, potentially even terminated it. But, with limited power, the pregnancy took hold.

"I'll figure it out."

"Okay," Bastet said, "I'll keep your secret for now, on one condition."

Sif's eyes narrowed. "What do you want?"

"I want to be there when you give birth. I want to see my little niece or nephew take their first breath."

Of all the demands Sif could have expected, Bastet's presence during the birth hadn't been one. Tears began to well in Sif's eyes.

"You're my best friend," she said, stopping a moment to sniff. "You were always going to be invited to the birth."

Bastet smiled. "Good."

"It's a boy, by the way," Sif said. "I'll have to talk to Apollo about names later tonight."

"We'd best be getting back to the party. People are going to start wondering where we went."

"One second."

Sif turned the tap on one of the three sinks and took a quick mouthful of water. She swished the water around before spitting it back into the sink. She fixed her hair and outfit before turning back to Bastet.

"All right," she said, "let's go."

When eight o'clock struck, the gods made their way to three long tables, reserved for each pantheon. The chairs lining the tables were engraved with the names of the gods, the placement of each chair carefully chosen to encourage conversation and avoid fighting. Athena chuckled in amusement when she saw Ares' place had been set as far from her as possible.

At the head of each table sat a chair for the heads of each pantheon. Toward the wall stood a large stage which would be the source of entertainment for the rest of The Gathering. Athena looked forward to the sparring matches between her, Ares, Thor and Sekhmet for the entertainment of the others, as well as the plays, poetry and speeches.

The first speech would come from the three kings before the banquet began. Athena looked across the table at Dionysus and studied his face. She could see the pride he felt as he waited in anticipation for all the gods to taste his food. He'd be congratulated for managing to adhere to every god's individual palate and still making the dishes look beautiful. She'd seen it happen time and time again.

Beside Athena sat Demeter and Hermes. They talked to the people beside them, as planned. Athena wasn't one for small talk, at least not normally. For the sake of being polite, she did what she could to partake as often as she could, though often failed. Demeter spoke with Artemis while Hermes talked to Apollo. Athena was left with her thoughts, as she preferred.

The lights grew dim as a telepathically-directed spotlight shone a brilliant white beam toward stage left. At once all three tables went silent, awaiting the speeches. Zeus walked from behind the blue curtain as a cheer erupted from the Olympians. The Asgardians were next as Odin emerged, and the cheering became louder as Ra came out shortly after.

Odin raised a hand parallel to his face; silence covered the hall as he closed it. He grabbed the microphone from the stand and looked over the room. Everyone could hear the long, drawn-out breath, captivated as the light reflected from his brilliant silver beard.

"Asgardians!" he shouted.

On cue, the Asgard table erupted into a series of war cries, each voice drowning the other out as they fought to express their pride. Odin looked to his people and flashed a grin. He raised his hand again and the cheers died down into silence.

"Another hundred years have passed," Odin said, more softly. The strength he held in his voice was only slightly counteracted by his age. "With each passing year, I feel myself humbled. Humbled by the knowledge I am still alive. Humbled, knowing if we had stayed as deities on Asgard, we'd have faded away by now.

"And yet, with every year that passes, I am also enraged for the choice I made all those years ago. I'd been given the chance to die with a sword in my hand; we all had. I took that away from all of you, and I cannot express how sorry I am to you, my fellow Asgardians, for stealing away your honourable deaths. Yes, one day we will all die of old age. Not soon enough, I might add.

"We've all worked our existence away for humanity, living very little as actual gods. Instead, we mingle among them. We've learned so much about the people of this world. We've watched them grow as a species from infancy into their poor teenage years. They have a long way to go, and we will continue to aid them along their way. Maybe someday they can become the beings they've always been meant to become.

"So, if I, if we *all*, are to die slow deaths; if we are not to die in the battlefield, but alone, let us die knowing we are working toward a noble cause. We may not rule them, but we will help them in every way we can." A small shimmer passed through Odin's eye. "For the glory of Asgard and all we do!"

The Asgardians raised their mugs in salute, each of them shouting at the top of their lungs. Athena noticed the only Asgardian not raising a glass was Sif. She didn't have a mug of mead in front of her. Instead she sipped a glass of water. Wonder crept through Athena's mind as she pondered why an Asgardian would drink water during a banquet, not to mention the only deity without any form of alcohol.

Her mind was taken away from Sif as Zeus slapped Odin on the back, grinning as he spoke. She couldn't hear a word he said but watched as he took the microphone. He said something to Ra before turning toward the tables.

"Olympians!" he shouted.

A cacophonous chorus of gods shouting "Haroom" in unison erupted from the table, Athena joining in. She could feel the camaraderie bonding her uncles, brothers and sisters as she shouted. It was the same feeling the Asgardians and Egyptians felt every Gathering. They were kin, they were together, and nothing could separate them.

Zeus waved his hand and silenced the Olympians.

"My charming brothers," he said gesturing toward Poseidon and Hades. "My darling wife," he said, gesturing to Hera, "and my beautiful children, welcome. I always love The Gatherings; they bring us together and remind us of who we are. Out there in the world, we live our own lives. We do what we can to benefit the human populace while contending with our own worlds.

"Some of us live meagre lives, content with the nine-to-five grind, while others insist on the spotlight. It is not for me or anyone else to judge how we live our lives, only that we live them with the utmost certainty and be the best we can.

"I know for a fact it doesn't matter the occupation we choose; we will always be best in the field. That said, we must allow for others to take the spot we so desire. We must stand aside and live humbly. For if we take all the glory for ourselves, there will be nothing for humanity to learn from.

"So, as we go on to our next hundred years, I want you all to make this vow."

Zeus placed his fist against his heart, and each member of the

Olympian table mirrored his action.

"I vow to stand aside. I vow to allow the humans to take the occupations I desire, for no other reason than to allow them to learn and grow for themselves.

"For the next hundred years! For Olympus!"

The Olympians raised their glasses and took mouthfuls of Ambrosia. The taste had always been difficult for Athena, or any Olympian, to describe. The flavour changed with each successive sip. What made the drink special was not the flavour, but the feelings it induced upon consumption. Waves of joy, depression and anger hit the brain at once, leaving Athena and each of the Olympians satisfied in their own ways.

Ra approached Zeus, said something Athena couldn't hear and took the microphone. She couldn't tell just how forceful the old sun god had been, but he didn't look as if he'd been gentle.

Ra had always been the sort of deity Athena avoided. In over two thousand years, she had never once seen him smile, or show any sort of emotion far from anger or some form of indescribable intensity. Ares may be over the top in his rage, Odin may have a grim outlook, the underworld gods may have a bit of obsession with death, but at least they managed to show more character than she'd ever seen from Ra. The one short conversation she'd had with him had brought only two words from his lips. She couldn't remember exactly what she'd said, but his response was 'Go away.' She never again tried to speak to him.

Ra looked out to the crowd with a deeper intensity than normal. The sun-disk balanced on his head didn't so much as wobble with any of his movements. She couldn't tell if it had been from impeccable balance or deity powers. It wouldn't have surprised her if the answer was both.

"Egyptians," he said in a low, domineering voice.

The Egyptian table remained silent; not one muscle so much as twitched under Ra's eye.

"It pleases me to see you all here. I had my worries when we all had dreams. Not for my own pantheon; mine is built of sturdier stuff than the over-happy Olympians or the desperate for death Asgardians. You've all made me proud.

"As the eldest of the current and surviving pantheons, it is our duty to watch over not only the humans we silently rule over, but the younger gods as well. We set the example for others to follow. Odin wants to die helping the humans, a noble cause and worthy of my respect. Zeus wants to help the humans by having them help themselves, a worthy cause.

"It is we, the Egyptians, who have taught such morals to our Olympian and Asgardian brethren. That is what they are, these men and women who share this room with you. They are your family. Such a belief has got me thinking, giving me ideas even fifty years ago I'd have never considered. We are to dissolve the differences between Asgardian, Olympian and Egyptian. I look out on the room and see a husband and wife who can't sit together because they're from different pantheons. I see gods who would prefer to sit together.

"To those who may be about to ask, no, I have not discussed this with Zeus or Odin. I wanted to see what they would tell their pantheons during their centennial speeches. I was not disappointed. What impressed me more, though, was all of you. Not just my Egyptians, but the Olympians and the Asgardians. This is the first gathering I've seen where I couldn't pick out one group with members of only one pantheon. Everyone has mixed together, and it pleases this old god's heart to see it.

"Some of you might be thinking — hell; I know Apophis and Set are thinking I've gone soft. I've become sentimental in my old age. That could be true. But don't think I won't be the person the gods need me to be at any given moment.

"So, Egyptians, Olympians, Asgardians, stand tall as elder gods. Stand as brothers and sisters, stand as one, for if we do, nothing can—"

Ra's words were cut short by the sound of a single set of hands clapping. The gods all turned their heads toward the door to see five winged figures in the doorway.

"Michael," Athena said under her breath.

Michael's hands stilled, his grin stretching farther than any mouth conceivably should.

"Moving speech," he said. "Don't let me stop you. After all, you will never have another Gathering."

"What the fuck are you talking about?" Zeus asked.

Michael's grin vanished in an instant; in its place laid a scathing sneer.

"What I mean is, you're leaving Earth — by your own choice, or in a body bag. Either way is fine with me."

Odin shook his head.

"Yahweh guaranteed us safety on earth for as long as our deific lives allowed. We left our pantheons for this."

"My father is gone," Michael snapped. "Has been for almost fifty years. I don't know where he is, and by now I think it's safe to say he's not coming back. You know what that means? It means I'm in charge. You know what else? That means any contract he made with you lot is null and void, including your safety here on Earth. I don't want to share my plane with a bunch of old gods who think they're better than the ruling deity. I know you thought yourselves better than my father, and you'll think the same of me. You might even try your hand at overthrowing me."

"We would never —" Zeus began.

"I'm not taking that chance," Michael said. "Rules have been broken, and I can't allow you all to regain your godly powers. I will happily escort you all to a safe place, a whole new plane of existence where you can live as gods once again. You'll be supervised by my angels, obviously, but you'll be permitted to live freely and create as you wish. You just can't stay here. You'll have until daylight tomorrow to make up your minds."

"Do you honestly think you can beat us?" a woman from the Egyptian table asked.

"Who are you?" Michael asked.

She puffed out her chest. "My name is Isis, widow of Osiris, holder of the true name of Ra and -"

Before she could finish her sentence, an arrow of light passed through her skull, between her eyes and out the back of her head. Athena watched in horror as the goddess's eyes widened, as her brain fought to recognise what had happened. A moment later, her head crashed on the table before falling to the floor.

"Just the name would have worked," Michael spat. "Like I said, you have until daylight to decide. Choices will be taken on an individual basis. If some want to stay and fight, or if the majority want to fight, I'll be happy protect those who want to live. We'll wholesale slaughter the rest."

Upon the last syllable, Michael and the angels vanished in a flash of white light. Silence followed as the gods stared at one another. Nobody knew what to make of the situation, nor how to cope with the ultimatum.

Finally, Zeus spoke.

"If anybody wants to go, please do. You will not be looked down upon. I, for one, am going to fight these assholes with everything I've got."

"Why, though?" Demeter asked, sounding as if she were baiting the answer rather than asking the question.

"One very simple reason," Zeus said. "Because it will never end. Yahweh told us we can live here on Earth. We've been living here for a thousand years. To many of you, this has been your home longer than you'd lived within your pantheon. Now, because Michael is having a hissy fit over his daddy leaving, we have to move? I don't fucking think so. After all, what's to stop Michael or any of the archangels from attacking us within the separate plane? What's to stop them from pushing us around? No. I say we stand and fight. We show those cocksuckers what we're made of and die defending our home."

Zeus stopped for a moment to take in a deep breath. "Who's with me?"

The hall erupted with cheers from every god and goddess in the room. Athena clapped with vigor along with many others. Come daybreak, the war would begin. Athena didn't expect to survive; she didn't expect the gods to win. She did expect to make Michael's victory as pyrrhic as possible.

She watched the stage as Odin and Ra approached Zeus and stood with him. Athena's smile widened; Ra's wish was coming true. It wasn't in the way he expected, but the Olympians, Asgardians and Egyptians would all be working together.

Chapter 5

Hephaestus ran as quickly as his crippled foot would allow. The sound of his cane echoed through the alley as he scampered between the brick buildings. His breathing was hard and rough; years of breathing fumes from human metals had given his lungs a thorough beating. His two packs a day didn't help.

He knew he couldn't fight; to do so would require mobility, something he didn't have. Hiding himself away was his only option. He wished he'd been able to go to the plane the angels offered, but when nobody moved, he knew he couldn't be the only coward in the room. Zeus's words stirred a feeling within him, a pride he hadn't felt for much too long.

When he'd left the hall, his terror returned. He'd never been a fighter; he'd always been more comfortable creating the weapons than using them. Ares had tried to teach him to use a sword a long time ago, a sort of apology for what happened between them and Aphrodite. Hephaestus couldn't move like Ares or the others, and failed at weaponry.

An angel flew down from the top of a building. He didn't move as it descended and landed a foot away. Hephaestus lowered his shoulders, "I don't want to fight you," he said.

The angel looked him up and down, its face never changing.

"No? I thought all you gods were proud and unwilling to accept Michael's offer."

Hephaestus closed his eyes and shook his head.

"I'm not a fighter, I'm a smith. I can't fight. So, I'm going to take Michael up on his offer. I'll go to his new plane of existence and live out the rest of my days there."

A slight smile formed on the angel's face. "Very well."

In a flash, the angel produced a glowing, blue blade. Hephaestus didn't have time to react as the blade passed through his middle. Agony flashed through his body for a fleeting moment before the wound went numb. He looked down to see the rich red blood pouring from his abdomen.

"What?" was the only word he managed to say before he fell to the ground.

"You're a bit dense, aren't you?" the angel said. "There never was another plane of existence. Michael doesn't have that sort of power; he'd have to become a full-fledged deity to do that. But at least I got to kill one of you without a fight."

Hephaestus looked on helplessly as the angel hovered the edge of the blade over his throat. The angel raised the blade, and in a fluid swing Hephaestus felt his head separate from his body.

Tyr ran along the city streets, sword in hand, a shield attached to the arm missing the other hand. His breathing remained steady, his eyes scanning every inch of his surroundings. He wasn't about to be jumped by an angel unprepared for the fight.

He placed a silent step down on the street, wondering if the local human populace would take notice of the battle around them. It was doubtful; most humans rarely noticed the ongoing matters of the higher beings around them. If one, or any, did happen to notice something strange, it was likely they would shrug it off and continue as if nothing had happened. It would only be those caught in the crossfire that would see the fight, and they wouldn't get the chance to tell the tale.

He could feel the wind on the back of his neck, making the small hairs stand on end.

He sniffed, hoping to catch the scent of myrrh and petrichor; the scent of an angel. As expected, he could smell one nearby. His eyes narrowed as he continued to sniff the air, trying to narrow down where the winged creature would be.

Tightening his grip on the sword, Tyr walked to an empty office building. He brought his blade down on the door, slicing the lock in half. The door opened slightly on its own, and Tyr used the blade of the sword to open it the rest of the way.

The building was dark, the perfect place to hunt an angel. The angel's natural glow would prevent anything like an ambush. He'd spot the angel and kill it before it had the opportunity to take him down.

Following the scent, he entered the stairwell and ascended. Floors passed him as he climbed the stairs slowly, careful to follow the scent as accurately as possible. By the time he arrived at the fifteenth floor, the scent had become strong. He opened the door and walked into the darkness.

Scent wouldn't be much help in such proximity; he kept his eyes trained on anything that produced any sort of light.

"You might as well come out," Tyr growled. "I know you're here. You might as well die with honour, not as a coward."

Tyr heard a sigh from the far end of the room. A glowing figure stood up from behind a line of cubicles and walked toward the Norse deity.

"How did you find me?"

"You don't know? I thought you were trying to ambush me."

The angel laughed. "Not as such. I didn't think anyone would be in here. I was hiding."

"So, you are a coward," Tyr spat.

"No," the angel said, "I just don't want to have to kill gods, or anyone for that matter. I'm compelled to follow Michael's orders, which are to kill any god I see. If I don't see any gods, I don't have to kill them."

"And now?"

The look the angel gave Tyr made his heart sink. He'd just condemned the pacifistic angel to death, one who refused to fight unless his orders compelled him to. Tyr readied his sword and raised his shield as the angel pulled a glowing blue blade from his chest.

"I'm sorry," the angel said.

"It is my apologies you deserve," Tyr said. "This is on me."

The angel lunged at Tyr, the point of the blade positioned to pierce the Asgardian's heart. Tyr shifted his shield, blocking the attack; he flicked his wrist, sending his sword through the angel's wing. The sound the angel made as it screamed shattered several of the surrounding computer screens. Tyr's ears, however, remained unaffected.

The angel hadn't expected Tyr to land a hit. Its face glowed red and the eyes narrowed as rage filled the pure being's heart.

It swung at him again, and again and again. Each swing was precise, trained and coordinated with every movement of the angel's body to hit something vital of Tyr's. He'd expected a fight, but nothing of this calibre; he'd have to finish the fight as quickly as he could before the angel got lucky and landed a killing blow.

Tyr pushed the angel away with his shield, stealing a glance at the heavily chipped wood. It wouldn't be much for protection if the battle continued. He hoped it could take one more hit. Just one more blow and his victory would be ensured.

Tyr watched his opponent, took note of its every movement, no matter how slight. The angel rushed him again, its speed and accuracy astounding.

Before the angel's blade could connect with his shield, Tyr dropped low, forcing the edge of the shield into the angel's foot. It grimaced in agony as it struck again, connecting with the shield. Tyr was certain it saw the sword coming but couldn't do anything to stop it. Tyr's sword entered the angel through the groin and exited inches below the left shoulder blade, slicing the angel's heart in half.

As it lost footing and started to slump to the ground, Tyr caught the angel and gently set it down. "May the next world be kinder to you than this one."

FALLEN GODS

He watched as the angel slowly dispersed into light particles and soon was completely gone. Tyr picked up his sword and sheathed it. He used his power to fix his shield before heading back to the stairwell.

Set should have been enjoying the battles taking place around him. The chaos, sorrow and rage around the city filled him with energy, the sort he would have cherished a millennium before. As he stood atop the National Bank of Red City, all he felt was melancholy.

It wasn't that such things no longer excited him; it was that he wasn't the cause of the negative emotions. He'd been good and kept to himself for the most part during his time on Earth. The last thing he needed was the attention of Yahweh or any of his angels. He had no desire to be killed by a race of gods he deemed less worthy than the Asgardians or Olympians.

He sat in his chair, awaiting an angel's attack knowing it would come sooner or later. However, the longer he waited, the more thoughts of his own safety crept into his mind. It wasn't a realistic thought, He'd openly defied the angels; they would be coming for him. For the time being, he'd do his best to enjoy himself, despite the depression.

He'd considered becoming a turncoat; it wouldn't have surprised anyone if he had. He could have killed several of the other gods before they cut him down, or an angel or six came for him. He pictured himself fighting and killing as many gods and angels he could, deception being his friend. He pictured the killing blow and his laughter echoing into his final breaths.

He whimpered as he thought of Osiris. He'd hated his brother for so long, even after his resurrection. Set had sliced Osiris into ribbons and sent the pieces everywhere; it was all in good fun, though nobody took it that way. Sure enough, to Set's dismay, Isis had fixed him up, except for the one part Set intentionally fed to Sobek, the crocodile god. Osiris and Isis had both been livid when they realized his genitals couldn't be retrieved.

Having been sewn together, Osiris hadn't survived becoming

human. His body leaked and died almost instantly. To Set, it was one thing to cut up Osiris while he was a god and could be brought back; and while Osiris had a change of job, he was all the better for it. Permanent death, though, that was something Set didn't handle well.

Set turned away from the city and sat in his camping chair. He reached into the cooler beside him, pulled out a beer, lifted the tab and took in the scent of the fermented hops and barley.

"This is for you Osiris. You would have had a field day with these clowns," Set said.

He brought the can to his lips and let the cool beverage flow down his throat, drinking the entire contents of the can at once. He crushed the can under his foot and belched. He tossed the can behind him and pulled out another.

"This is for all the gods fighting for their lives, probably soon to include me, too."

He drank the third full can of beer, the effects of the alcohol starting to give him a happy buzz.

"One more," he said pulling another can out. "This one is for me, and all the chaos and mayhem I could have caused. If I hadn't been so goddamn scared, I just might have."

He emptied the can and threw it behind him. When he stood, his legs wobbled a little.

He grinned. "Excellent."

Set walked out to the edge of the roof. He stared back out at Red City, eyes narrowed, head swimming.

"All right," he said, "come and get me." Set raised his arms wide, prepared for whatever might happen. "Come on!" he screamed into the night, "Come and get me! I'm right here, an easy target! Come on! Come and get me!"

"This is the one place I don't think they can sense us," Bastet said, closing the doors to the church.

"Are you sure?" Sif asked, her belly clearly showing her pregnancy.

Bastet leaned her head to the side. "Not a hundred percent, if I'm being honest. But it's the best bet. They would see this little place and only feel their father's essence. Small church indicates Yahweh. Typically that's how it works, from what I've seen."

Sif nodded, turning to sit in pew. She looked up at the large statue of Jesus at the head of the church. He was a good kid, a little more sanctimonious than she liked, but he hadn't meant anybody any harm.

"Do you think if we pray, Yahweh will show up and explain what the fuck is going on?"

Bastet giggled. "I doubt it. I'm sure Michael's tried that more than enough times. Shit, I'm sure if he really wanted to come to us, he'd have shown himself already."

"Yeah, I'm sure you're right."

"I know I'm right."

The corner of Sif's mouth curled into a small, warm smile.

"You're my best friend, you know that, right?"

"Of course I do, and you're mine." Sif watched Bastet's face; she was suspicious. "Why did you need to say it?"

"It's nothing."

"Bullshit, you're thinking something. I want to know what it is."

Tears began to fall from Sif's eyes. Her husband was out there, fighting with the other gods. His face when she'd told him she was pregnant would have been hilarious at any other time, in any other circumstance. Given what had happened at The Gathering, his look was foreboding and one of stone-cold duty.

"I'm going to kill the angels," he said, his voice hard.

"No, please stay. I need you to keep me safe. I can't fight like this."

"Bastet," Apollo said, "keep her safe. Keep them both safe."

Bastet had nodded and said, "I will. You have my word."

"Come back to me," Sif said, tears beginning to well in her eyes.

"You know I will. I have too much to live for to die."

No more words were said until Apollo had been close to leaving. Bastet led Sif to a small church she'd known about and there they stayed, sitting in the pews in silence, careful not to attract any unwanted attention. Bastet had been sure to tell Apollo where they'd be hiding, just in case.

Boredom set in after a couple hours. Churches had never been known for their entertainment value and several hours in a small room with only a book of stories about the god they wanted nothing to do with had been excruciating.

"Do you think Apollo is all right?" Sif asked.

Bastet shook her head and wrapped her arms around Sif.

"You can't ask that question," she cooed, running her fingers through Sif's hair to calm her.

"I know," Sif said with a sniff "It's just hard being trapped in here while he's out there. I was a warrior; I could hold my own against damn near anything that came my way. Why couldn't Aphrodite get pregnant? She's not a fighter. I really just . . . I just wish I knew if he's okay or not."

"You can't question him and his abilities. You must know in your heart that he will survive for you. He knows if he dies, he fails you. He knows if he dies, he fails the baby, and if I know Apollo, he won't let that happen."

"You're right," Sif said, "but this is battle, anything can happen. I've seen great warriors fall to people who had no right being anywhere near a battlefield. Sometimes it's just the right place, right time; or vice versa."

"Do you think we're going to lose the fight?" Bastet asked.

Sif nodded, ashamed of her answer.

"We can kill as many angels as we need, but once the seven archangels come in, we're done for. We can't fight them."

"Not without our weapons," Bastet agreed. "But, if we can get the weapons, maybe we can win."

"That's an interesting thought," a voice from behind them said.

Sif and Bastet turned to see a man standing behind them, appearing to be in his early thirties. He wore a leather jacket over a white t-shirt and jeans. His pitch-black hair was styled into an organised mess.

"Oh, don't let me distract you," he said. "I was just listening in, thinking that if you had your weapons, you'd actually stand a chance against the archangels."

"Who are you?" Bastet asked, readying herself for attack.

"Really? You haven't figured it out? Like at all? Fuck, I thought you deities were supposed to be smart. This is what I get for dealing with the warrior princess and a cat. Where's that artsy Greek guy? I'm sure he'd figure it out right quick."

"Who are you?" Sif asked, not as forcefully as Bastet.

"You're not even going to try and guess?" He sighed. "Fine, I guess there's no point in wasting time. I'm Lucifer."

"The devil?" Bastet asked.

"Yes," Lucifer said, clearly frustrated. "The devil, Satan, El Diablo and whatever other silly names the church is calling me these days."

"Are you here to . . ."

"Kill you?" Lucifer shook his head, "Not at all my dear, I'm actually here because I want to help you."

"Help us?" Sif asked, surprised.

"Why should we trust you?" Bastet asked. "Aren't you supposed to be the Father of Lies or something?"

Sif watched as Lucifer's face contorted from mild amusement into a spiteful sneer.

"You've been listening to humans too long. As if they know a single fucking thing that goes on in any other plane than their own personal lives.

"Do you want to know the truth? It doesn't matter; I'm going to tell you anyway. It's a great story and I think more people need to know the truth. Besides, I'm tired of people not trusting me.

"One day, father called four of us up. We were the archangels he deemed the best of the best and most likely to succeed with the job he had. He told us he needed someone to take over the place where the dead dwell. At the time, it was basically nothing more than a pit filled to near capacity with souls. And he was straight with us. We'd never be able to return and humanity would hate us. There would be a few who would find sympathy for whoever took the job, but most would fear him. Any death god can explain how that feels.

"But there was a plus side. The angel would have total dominion over the land of the dead and be able to shape it as he wished. And, best of all, he'd be beyond my father's power. An archangel not bound by the Ten Commandments or the sins. So long as whoever was chosen did the job, which was to separate the souls from the good, bad and average, and if the job was done properly, Father would be pleased, and everything would be great.

"Michael refused. He couldn't stand to have father out of his sight for even a second. Based on the hissy fit he's throwing now, I'd say nothing's changed.

"Gabriel — and don't get me wrong, I like Gabriel, he's much nicer than people give him credit for — also refused, knowing he wouldn't be able to handle the job. The humanity part didn't bother him so much but having to damn people to torment did. He knew he couldn't handle it. I respect that as much now as I did then.

"As for Raphael . . .well, let's just say I agreed to do it before he had the chance to say yes."

"Why?" Bastet asked.

"Could you imagine that psychopath in charge of the souls of the dead? Everyone would be guilty, and I don't think he'd let them out once they'd atoned. The shit part is, my father knew it would be me running the show down there. It had to be; I was the only one independent enough, responsible enough and had the stomach to do what had to be done. He just didn't want it to look like I was being railroaded into it. That old man, he sure loves the illusion of choice over actual choice."

"Okay," Sif said, slowly and calmly, "but why do you want to help us?"

"Well, it's like this. I was more than happy to just watch Michael parade himself around Heaven and be the pompous ass he is. It would have been funny. But then he had to go after you lot, and that doesn't sit well with me."

"Didn't think you cared that much," Bastet said, scowling.

"Make no mistake, I don't," Lucifer said, "But, if he's willing to go after you, he'll eventually come after me"

Lucifer sighed. "A while back, maybe three hundred years or so ago, I'd have happily handed the keys over to Hell, or The Underworld or whatever you want to call it. The whole naming thing is convoluted.

"But, in these modern days, I love my job. Things are challenging and I have to think about where people go. I'm not going to let Michael take this away from me."

"So, you're doing this out of your own self-interest," Sif said.

"As are you," Lucifer shot back. "You're not doing it for me, my father's, or the human's self-interests. Glass houses, Sif."

Bastet grumbled to herself while Sif stiffened.

"We're fighting for our survival!"

"Bullshit," Lucifer said, "You had the opportunity to go to a whole new plane of existence. You all chose to stay behind. You're looking after your own self-interest. There isn't a new plane of existence anyway, but you couldn't have known that until I told you. You made the right choice, but let's not dress up the choice in the guise of altruism."

"You said you wanted to help," Bastet said, changing the subject. "How do you plan to do that?"

Lucifer grinned, "Simply put, I'm going to take three of you into Hell with me. To grab your weapons."

"Who?" Sif asked.

Lucifer paused, his brow furrowing, "That's the tricky part. It's really not for me to decide. If I were doing this just for fun, it wouldn't matter. But I have stakes in this battle, and there are rules even I have to abide by. So, I have to bring the whole lot of you, or at least those still alive, to a secret place where they can judge and determine who would be fit to accompany me." Lucifer paused and scratched the back of his head. "But, before I can allow entry, they have to be, um, appeased let's say."

"Who?" Bastet asked.

"Trust me, they're completely objective. They predate all of us in their own ways. Plus, the archangels are scared shitless of them, so you'll be safe while you're there."

"Who?" Sif asked, her voice holding more power than she'd managed in a long time.

Lucifer cleared his throat.

"The Four Horsemen of the Apocalypse."

Chapter 6

The stones of Olympus trembled with every step Zeus took. He wasn't supposed to be there, and the mountain knew it. Zeus had believed if he remained on the physical plane and touched as little of it as possible, he'd be able to climb the mountain.

Once he'd past the flora that coated the bottom half of the mountain, he could feel the rocks begin to give way under his feet. Zeus cursed; he'd used a lot of his power to arrive at the foot of Olympus. If the rocks were to give way fully under his feet, he'd be caught in a rockslide. He wouldn't die, but the rocks would leave him broken until he could regain enough power to heal and get out from under the rocks. By that time, his children, wife and brothers would all be dead.

He stepped as lightly as possible, keeping himself partially suspended in a semi-float. He wouldn't be able to hold it for the full trip, but he knew if he could reach the summit, he'd be safe. The mountain wouldn't come crashing down all at once, just from him being there.

His mind drifted to Odin and Ra. Their pantheons didn't have any specific homes in the mortal realm; all they needed was to reach where they had hidden their greatest threats and work from there. Neither would have it easy, though Zeus, decided he had the toughest task.

He wished it had been possible for him to have arrived in Greece upon the summit, saving himself a harrowing climb. He sucked in a lungful of oxygen and forced it into his bloodstream, feeding his brain and muscles. He was running out of power, and he was near the top.

His power gave out three steps later, forcing his foot to rest firmly on the ground. The mountain trembled and shook. The towns on the mountain would feel it and fear a rockslide. If one happened, none would escape in time. Zeus placed one foot in front of the other and raced headlong toward the summit.

He could see it ahead where the sky began. Step after step the rocks rumbled under him and fell to pieces. He reached out, and with a godly leap he landed at the summit.

Zeus looked over the Grecian landscape, marvelling at its beauty. A shard of lament tugged at his heart as he wished he'd appreciated his home more when he'd still had the power to make a difference.

With a sigh, Zeus raised his hands, palms down. For the first time, for almost as long as his body could remember, he spoke ancient Greek.

"Typhon, youngest son of Gia, son of Tartarus, love of Echidna and father of the great monsters of old, I command you to rise. I, Zeus, king of the gods of Olympus, summon you to the mount's summit. The time has come for us to speak, to strike the bargain foretold. Rise, Typhon. Be temporarily free of your prison and rise."

Dark clouds formed over the landscape, casting shadows around Zeus. He felt the mountain rumble as Typhon broke from his restraints. Zeus could only imagine the damage the beast was causing in what was left of Tartarus. Fear gripped Zeus's brain as he began to justify his actions. Typhon was a horror to mankind, the sort who could cause a lot of damage if Zeus didn't plan things and use the correct words to make a binding contract.

Abruptly, the rumbling ceased, leaving an eerie calm in the air around the summit. The clouds began to shift and focus into a single area, slowly taking the form of a serpent. The tail stretched nearly a kilometre in length before a torso took shape. Zeus watched as abs, pecs and shoulders took shape, followed by two large arms and massive furled wings. The head was the final creation, taking the general shape of a man's skull with the face of a snake.

Once the clouds had made their form, Typhon emerged with a crash of lighting erupting around him.

"*Zeus,*" the serpent hissed. "*Why have you summoned me?*"

Zeus drew in a breath as he attempted to hold his composure. If Typhon tried anything, he would be powerless to stop the beast. His best bet would be to bluff, and hope Typhon couldn't tell.

"*I've come to make a bargain with you.*"

A plume of dark smoke drifted from Typhon's nostrils.

"*I'm going to assume that you are the one who allowed me to be reunited with my darling Echidna. For that, I will not kill you where you stand and will hear your bargain. Speak quickly, old god. I don't have forever. And from what I can see, neither do you.*"

Zeus cleared his throat.

"*The gods of Olympus require the aid of your children.*"

Typhon's eyes widened as he drew his head back. Whatever Zeus could have said, it appeared as if he hadn't expected that. Zeus hadn't expected Typhon to release a low growled laugh in response.

"*You require my children's aid? Have the gods of Olympus grown so weak they need the help of monsters who were at one time killed by mere men?*"

"*Not at all, Typhon. We Olympians are few, while the angels are many; we merely plan to use them to keep the angels distrac —*"

"*You can't fool me, elder god,*" Typhon hissed. "*The climb has weakened you terribly. If the great Zeus is this weak, it's a marvel your children and brothers still live. But let it not be said I didn't come to the aid of the Gods of Olympus in their hour of need.*"

"*Thank you,*" Zeus said.

Fire flashed from Typhon's eyes.

"*I'm not finished,*" he roared. "*Let it not be said I didn't come to the aid of Olympus in its hour of need. For it was inevitable Zeus would compensate Typhon greatly in thanks."*

"There it is," Zeus said, unsurprised at the catch. "What do you want?"

Typhon uncrossed his arms and pointed a giant finger at Zeus "You."

"Me? Anything else?"

Typhon shook his strange, massive head. *"Tartarus has been cozy since the gods and souls have left, more so since Echidna arrived. I do not desire true freedom. No, elder god, what I want is you. I wish to consume your flesh and absorb your power."*

Zeus sighed. "Well, here I am."

"Not as you are. You get your power back, and if you win, I get to eat you. This is my one and only demand. My children will obey you and your people while protecting them with their lives. If you win, and if you survive, you will be mine. I will choose how I eat you, be it quickly or slowly, painfully or painlessly."

Zeus's mouth began to hurt from gritting his teeth. He shot a burst of air from his nose and said, *"You have a deal Typhon. Send your monsters to the place I've sent to your mind. That's where the angels will be."*

"As you command, elder god," Typhon said, bowing his head.

Zeus sighed, hoping he'd made the right choice.

The cave had decayed as the years passed. Odin walked through what used to be a well-kept rocky prison, intended to hold the prisoners of Asgard. As the area wasn't a part of the Asgardian realm, he was able to safely enter and walk through. Zeus, however, would have had a difficult time on Olympus due to their home and the mountain being the same place.

Stalactites had formed from the ceiling, nearly reaching the ground. Odin walked past several before coming to a large boulder. Several rotted leather straps lay in near full decay at the bottom. The skeleton of a snake remained intact at the top, coiled within a small clay bowl. It had been where Loki had once been bound during his punishment for the death of Baldur.

The serpent had been suspended above Loki, dripping venom into his eyes. The bowl had been held by Loki's wife, Sigyn, to protect him from the venom. However, once the bowl filled, she'd have to empty it, leaving Loki's eyes open to the venom.

Odin shook his head. He had been a baron for punishment, doling it out as he saw fit. Mortals, gods and those from other worlds hadn't been safe from Odin's wrath. In his time among the mortals, he'd realized he'd grown humble, abhorring his actions as the All Father.

Odin narrowed his eyes and continued forward. His destination was much further into the cave, far deeper than any human dared venture.

In his head, a voice spoke.

"Am I going mad, or has the All Father returned?"

"It is I," Odin said telepathically. "I have returned."

He could feel the wolf's grin in his mind.

"Fascinating. I'd expected to die here," Fenrir said. "A thousand years without food is bound to make anyone hungry."

"We didn't really have a choice," Odin said. "We were banished from our homes."

"Yet here you are," Fenrir growled. "No banishment backlash, no problems or qualms. Someone could have come to feed me. Someone could have come to make sure everything was all right, but no, you all left. Tell me why I shouldn't just eat you here and now."

"Gleipnir will continue to hold unless I release you," Odin shot back.

"Or once Ragnarök begins."

"Ragnarök isn't going to come. The Christian invasion made sure of that."

"Then I shall be here forever," Fenrir's voice sounded less mighty.

Odin snarled as he continued forward.

"I'm not here to fight you," he said. "I'm here to make a deal with you."

"And why should I take this deal?"

Odin's snarl shifted into a sardonic smirk.

"Because I could just leave and allow you to starve to death. It's been a thousand years with an empty belly? How much longer do you think it'll take before you finally die? A hundred more years? Two? Five? Another thousand maybe? I can set you free, so long as you take the bargain."

Silence. Odin started to wonder if Fenrir would accept the possibility of a deal.

"All right," Fenrir said. "I'll hear you out. But, if I choose to decline the offer, you have to strike me down and end my pain."

Odin nodded. *"Deal."*

"Say what you have to say," Fenrir said.

Odin finally came to the room Fenrir was trapped in. He opened the door, careful not to spook the wolf within. Once he entered, he saw the great beast, lying with his head on his paws. Around its neck was the small ribbon, Gleipnir. The ribbon had been created by the dwarves when Fenrir had been foretold to be Odin's death. Attached to a slab and anchored with a stone, Fenrir remained tied.

Fenrir raised his head as Odin entered. *"Speak All Father. I wish for this to be finished."*

"The archangels are attacking, and we need your help to fend them off. You won't be able to kill the archangels, but you'll be able to kill and eat as many angels as you desire."

Fenrir's ears perked at the sound of food.

"Divine cuisine would be nice," Fenrir said, "but I'm afraid that won't be enough. I require more to take this offer, no matter how it intrigues me."

Odin scratched his beard, thinking about how to sweeten his offer.

"If we win, you get two souls a year."

"Human souls?"

"To devour and enjoy at your leisure."

"I can't help but notice you haven't offered yourself to the platter."

"Would you like to eat me?" Odin asked.

"No. Without the promise of Ragnarök, I see little point in devouring you. If the great cycle will not come to a close, you may as well continue to live." Fenrir paused for a moment, the wolf's lament becoming clear, "But this deal will involve you. I'll accept your deal of eating as many angels as I wish during the battle and your two souls a year. But, while I devour those souls, you must be present for the whole ordeal. I want you to experience what you're offering me. I want you to suffer by my maw. Eating you would be too fast, no matter how slowly I savour you. No, you get to watch, you have to watch. You can't look away; you must stare into the eyes of each soul I consume. My teeth tearing into their flesh, my saliva coating their skin, the horror in their eyes as they await permanent destruction; I want you, All Father Odin, to experience this. Do you take my side of the deal?"

Odin expelled a breath of air from his nose and nodded, his face as stony as Fenrir's bonds.

"I accept," Odin said.

Fenrir grinned as he stood. The wolf was twice the height of Odin, having grown considerably since they'd chained him. It was incredible Gleipnir hadn't strangled the wolf. Odin approached the ribbon, cautious to not get too close to Fenrir's jaws.

"You smell scared, All Father," Fenrir said, a hint of amusement in his voice. "I've already made the deal with you, neither of us can break it. Release me, so I may feed."

Odin sighed, placed his hand on the ribbon and willed the release. The moment he thought it, the ribbon came loose in his hands and Fenrir was gone.

Ra felt the hot sun on his skin as he walked the Egyptian desert. He soaked in the heat, feeling his power rising. His blood burned while his muscles tensed with every passing moment. Ra had come to love his home in Canada, but the frozen land was nowhere near what Egypt was to him.

He stopped once he hit the direct centre of the country. A stream of air passed through his nostrils before he raised his hands, placing his palms together. Lowering his hands to the centre of his chest, Ra released the pressure in is palms and creating a circle. He knelt, placing his hands in the burning sand. cupping the sand, he brought the grit over his head and allowed the grains to fall over his head.

"I, Ra, the self-created, God of the high noon sun, father of Shu, Tefnut, Hathor, Sekhmet, Bastet, Satet and Ma'at. I call upon you, my brother Sobek. I ask you for your aid in my conflict. Arise my brother, allow me your presence."

Ra pictured Sobek in his mind as he spoke. Immediately after, his mind shifted as he pictured Ammit.

"I, Ra, the self-created, God of the high noon sun also call upon Ammit. I require your presence, devourer of souls. I beg of you to arise and aid me in my conflict."

For several minutes, the desert remained still. No trace of wind caressed Ra's flesh; no sand moved beneath him. Even the sun in the sky appeared to be stuck in place. They were deciding.

Close by, sand began to shift. Ra turned to face the emerging beasts. Sobek was the first to arise. Ra stared at the giant bipedal crocodile, Sobek. The beast's jaw hung open as it glared at Ra. Ammit rose shortly after.

Ammit grinned, her crocodilian face displaying a wide array of teeth. Her head connected to a lion's mane and shoulders; just below, the fur ended and the back of a hippopotamus completed her body.

"Why have you called us?" Sobek growled.

Ra stood straight, his face straight and domineering.

"I have come to ask for your aid in the fight against the angels."

"You have a lot of nerve asking us for help," Ammit said in a low growl. "You abandoned us, Ra, left us in the desert to die."

"Tell us why we shouldn't just eat you," Sobek added. "You're weak, we could devour you quickly and easily."

"I didn't abandon you," Ra said, frowning. "I did leave with several other gods, yes. I don't deny that, nor will I apologise for it. The two of you were left behind because you couldn't blend with the humans. *You would have been hunted or killed. For your safety, and because I wanted nothing more than your comfort and for you to not lose your homes, I asked the angels to allow the two of you to remain in Egypt. My actions were not out of spite, but of kindness, love and concern."*

Sobek and Ammit said nothing. They looked to each other and peered down at Ra. Both towered over Ra, Ammit by double his height, Sobek by triple. Ra peered deeply into Sobek's eyes.

"I don't ask this of you lightly. I accept that you were hurt by our absence and my returning to ask for your help could be considered an insult."

"And yet you refuse to apologsze," Ammit growled. *"Is your pride so important?"*

"I will apologise for one thing," Ra said, his stance remaining strong. *"Not once did I ask either of you what you wanted. My intentions for the two of you were pure and caring. But I should have spoken with the two of you before taking everyone else away."*

Rage filled Sobek's eyes; he roared and lunged at Ra.

"You're weak! Ra does not apologise, Ra does not bow to the whim of others, Ra does not ask for help!"

Ra dodged Sobek's attack and stepped to the side. He summoned the energy he'd absorbed from the sun and hurled a fireball at Sobek's head. The crocodile god screamed and fell to the ground, black scorch marks visible between his scales.

"I may not be the god I used to be," Ra said, his voice elevated and booming, *"but my asking is nothing more than a professional courtesy. I could command you, and you'd do it. I want to give the two of you a choice. If you decline, so be it. The beasts of Asgard and Olympus will suffice. But, if you do choose to help, you will be rewarded with anything my power may allow. If we win, I will achieve full god status once again and can reward you with your desires."*

Ammit's face shifted from anger to a mischievous grin.

"You didn't say Olympus and Asgard had stakes in this."

"That changes everything", Sobek said, rising from the ground.

"*Will you help?*" Ra asked.

"*We will,*" Ammit said, "*on the condition that once we're done, Sobek and I will hold dominion over the remaining creatures.*"

Ra held his head high. "*I cannot honour that agreement.*"

Sobek nodded. "*We know, it was a test to see your desperation and honesty. You don't need us, but you want us. I'm in.*"

"*I am in as well,*" Ammit said, "*provided I get to take dominion over the underworld once finished.*"

"*I can honour that agreement,*" Ra said." Sobek, is there anything you wish for?"

"*I want a lake. Just a single lake all to myself. Those who come to the lake will be considered sacrifices to me and I'll accept them gracefully.*"

"*I can honour that agreement.*"

"*We should be off,*" Ammit said. "*I can feel my stomach growling, and only divine meat can satisfy this hunger.*"

Back in Red City, the angels came at Athena in hordes. Her jaw clenched as she thrust her spear into the breast of an angel. It died and vanished into a flash of white light. Behind her, Ares finished slaying two angels; their bodies bursting into light

Athena would have laughed had the situation not been so dire. She and Ares had been bitter rivals, both as gods of war, Athena specializing more in tactics while Ares brought pure chaos to combat. Against the attacking angels, there they stood, side by side. When they were gods, they'd have done everything in their power to kill one another. The irony of them helping each other stay alive was incredible.

"Above!" Ares shouted, positioning his shield.

Athena ran toward Ares, leaped onto his shield. Ares shot his arm upward as Athena jumped at the angel. She arched her arm and jabbed the spear at the angel, catching it in the throat. The angel released a pained gurgle before bursting.

She landed safely on the ground as several dozen more angels emerged, surrounding them.

"How many do you think there are?" Ares asked.

"I don't know, maybe fifty, maybe more."

The angels stared at the gods, ready to attack at any move. Ares snickered.

"Bet I kill more than you before we die."

Athena couldn't help but smirk. "You're on."

She raised her weapon and prepared for the oncoming attack. The angels glared from beneath their helms, looks of pure hatred and fear meeting her gaze.

"Well," Athena said, "What are you waiting for? Come at me!"

She lunged at an angel as a piercing scream filled the park. Athena looked toward the sound, seeing a sight she hadn't seen in a very long time. A reptile with a long neck grabbed an angel with its jaws. The newly reborn hydra's foot-long fangs impaled the divine creature, killing it.

Athena watched, noticing the dead angel didn't vanish. Instead, the light surrounding the divine being faded. The hydra's single head gnawed on the angel's corpse, sending the other angels into a fury. The hydra threw the angel aside and began snapping at the angels flying around it, catching some, but missing most.

Athena and Ares took the distraction as a chance to attack what angels they could while gaining some distance from the beast. One of the angels managed to cut the hydra's head off, leaving the body slack as it fell to the ground. One by one, the angels turned back to face Ares and Athena.

Athena inhaled deeply as they landed on the ground.

"Clever," an angel said, "using a monster to attack us. Your beast is dead now, as you will soon be."

Out of nowhere, two angels screamed as the hydra took two of them in two of its mouths. The angels turned, some screamed. "What the?" one said before the jaws clamped around it.

The angels began slicing at it, careful not to remove any more heads. Athena didn't think the beheading hydra tactic would work more than once, though surprisingly the hydra looked to have also expected the angels to not fall for the same trick twice.

Athena stabbed an angel and got a glimpse of the hydra as one of its heads attempted to snatch angels from the air. Surprise struck her as she saw the other head thinking, strategizing. The head on the right nodded as the left head lunged at the right's neck at the base. It tore the head off and proceeded to attack the angels as two more heads grew back.

The angels flew back into Ares's and Athena's weapons. The hydra continued to rip its own heads off, causing more to grow back. Before Athena knew what was happening, twelve heads snapped and grabbed angels from the sky.

The angels screamed as they tried to kill the hydra, but each wound healed as fast as they could hit it. Several of the hydra's heads cackled as the others bit down on the last of the angels. Once dead, the hydra began to peel the armour from the fallen and consume their flesh.

Athena took a step back as the scent of brimstone filled her nostrils.

"Ares?" she said, "Do you smell that?"

Ares grunted "Something is wrong."

They didn't get the chance to answer their query as they burst into flames and in seconds they were gone, leaving only the hungry hydra behind.

Of all things, Michael hadn't expected the gods to use monsters. He'd expected several them to defy him and fight while some would be slaughtered as traitors. To his knowledge, only one had tried to take the deal; the rest fought or accepted their fate.

In the distance he could see Set, standing on a rooftop with his arms stretched out. He was calling for his death, waiting for an angel to finish him off. Michael grinned as he decided Set would be last. He would get to experience the deaths of everyone he knew before succumbing to the blade.

Below, he watched as a giant wolf tore angels to shreds, two under each paw and three in its massive jaws. Farther in the city, a giant bipedal crocodile ate angels mercilessly. Monsters ran everywhere, taking over the city, only obeying those who had summoned them.

Michael glowered at the thought that his angels would go through true death at their hands. The weapons the gods held were not powerful enough to truly kill angels, only banish their forms back to Heaven for a short while. The monsters ensured permanent death through the sorts of acts Michael hated witnessing.

He sighed; he'd hoped to avoid releasing the archangels into the city. He wanted the fighting to remain unnoticed by the populace of Red City. From where he stood, it was no longer an option. He needed to be able to slay the monsters before they could lose the war for him.

He feared the monsters would get in lucky hits and kill the archangels around him. With only seven in the pantheon, each archangel was essential for his war. He screamed in frustration before calming himself and placing his hands together.

"Dear brothers, I summon you, the archangels, to Red City."

Chapter 7

A dull red haze enveloped Athena's vision as the scent of brimstone and fire filled her nose and heat scorched her flesh. The haze eventually receded, revealing a large domed arena. Glowing crimson stone lined the walls to the ceiling. A tight rope, suspended three feet from the wall and chest high, separating the arena from the spectators.

One by one, gods began to appear around her — Ares, Khonshu, Hathor, Loki, Thor, Artemis, Demeter — and they kept coming. When the procession stopped, she noted how many were missing. Several Egyptians were gone, along with a few Asgardians; yet only Hephaestus and Aphrodite were missing from the Olympians.

"The fuck?" Set said from across the arena. "Where am I?"

"Where are *we*, is a better question," Apollo said, looking around.

"We're in the underworld," Hades said, his voice grim. "Well, an adjacent area set off from the underworld. That's why we death gods can be here."

Athena watched as Apollo spotted Sif and Bastet and moved toward them. Athena then looked to Ares who shrugged; he didn't know what was going on either.

"Good evening, everyone," a disembodied voice said, filling the arena. "I'm sorry to have dragged all of you from your fight, but I believe this to be a matter of the utmost urgency."

An archangel formed before them, one Athena knew of well.

"Some of you may not know me; I'm Lucifer. Now, I know what you're thinking. 'Lucifer? He's the devil! What could he possibly want with us?' And, to put it simply, I have your weapons; and I want to give them to you."

Sekhmet snorted. "If you could have, you would have already."

"Unfortunately, that's not the case. As you all should well know, the weapons are locked away in a chest, only accessible if one from each of the three pantheons are present to open it. I can't even touch it. Whatever you lot did to it, it repels archangels. A clever move, but troublesome given the circumstance."

"So what?" Artemis said. "You're here to take three of us to Hell to get our weapons?"

Lucifer snapped his fingers and pointed to Artemis.

"Bingo! But I can't choose who goes, and neither can you.."

"What?" Tyr asked. "What do you mean?"

"I'm immune to a lot of the rules the archangels have to follow, leaving me free to do as I wish, to an extent," Lucifer said "My father's contract with you may or may not be still in effect ; it's a little shaky with his disappearance. As such, certain rules still apply. And, since Hell is a metaphysical plane of existence, much like your own underworlds, it counts as a place you can't go.

"But there are those who are capable of, countermanding my father's contract with you. They will be the ones to choose who goes to retrieve your weapons. I will say right here and now, though, that no underworld deities can go. They've made that point quite clear, so don't get your hopes up if you don't want to go down there. If they pick you, you're going."

Once Lucifer finished speaking, four shapeless forms emerged from the floor. They flew around the room several times before finally coming to a standstill in the centre of the arena. Lucifer looked at the forms for a moment before turning back to the gods.

"Ladies and gentlemen, gods and goddesses, it pleases me to

introduce to you the Four Horsemen of the Apocalypse. Okay, Horsemen might be a bit of an inaccuracy considering they don't ride horses, but it's what people know them as. They're more of a set of concepts embodied. I'm rambling, let's do this."

Athena gaped in awe as the shapeless apparitions shifted between several forms of reality at once. Slowly, they began to change colour and faded into a blue-white hue. A moment passed before one of the forms flew to the ground, turned a blood red and began to take physical shape. Two legs emerged as the apparition developed a nude torso. Arms and a head soon took shape. The face was boyish until hair began to sprout, giving it a fully formed beard. Age and rage were present within its stone grey eyes, as crimson armour emerged from its skin.

The being let out a long breath and spoke "Greetings, I am War."

"I'm a god of war," Ares sneered. "Sekhmet there is a god of war, there are several gods of war. What makes you so special?"

War grinned, showing a set of pointed teeth. The image sent a shiver down Athena's spine.

"Yes, you are a god of war," he said. "I, however, am what compels you to fight. I'm the inspiration for war, I'm the cause of war, I'm the warrior within the war. I *am* war. I'm every battle, both big and small. When you, Ares, fight, you are a part of me. I arrive when the battle begins and leave once it ends. You take sides; I do not, for I cannot. Without me, you would have no purpose."

Lucifer cleared his throat as loudly as he could. War stopped speaking and looked to the archangel of the underworld.

"All right," he said casually, "If all the pointless posturing is done, I believe we have deals to make. I'm under the impression that time is of the essence, so we should really get going ."

War nodded in agreement before Lucifer continued.

"So, each Horseman will have a specific thing they want. Once they are appeased, they will make the decision as to who goes into the underworld with me. Before we begin, are we all in agreement?"

Athena nodded without thinking. Without their weapons they

were as good as dead; it was best to appease the Horsemen as best they could to give themselves a fighting chance. She watched several other gods give their approval, while others looked as if they still needed convincing.

Lucifer gazed at the gods, disappointment clear on his face. "This has to be unanimous," he said. "Even if one of you disagrees, I'll have to send you all out there without your weapons and all of our time will be wasted and you will all die."

A few more gods nodded in agreement. Only one sat in disagreement.

"Set," Athena said, "why are you fighting this?"

"We've had our reign, we've had our lives," he said. It's time for someone else to take over."

"Is your life so inconsequential that you're willing to let everyone die for your stubbornness?"

"It's not that."

"What is it then?"

"We were gods once, and let's face it, we were not the sort of deities the humans deserved. We were so much worse. We put them through Hell with our petty squabbles; we punished them for minor infractions or for daring to compare themselves to us. We were terrible deities who had no right ruling humanity. They gave us our weapons; we are that much closer to becoming full gods again. History repeats itself and we are bound to become what we once were."

Athena leaned toward the Egyptian, "Set, I see where you're coming from, and I agree. I really do. We were terrible to humans, all of us. Aphrodite basically started the Trojan War, because she liked the idea of Paris and Helen being together. You Egyptians tended to be absent in your people's affairs. Odin and Loki were known to trick people for their own reasons. Thor held a 'strike first don't bother with questions' philosophy. Hera was a vengeful shrew. We were not good.

"But the time we've spent on Earth with the humans taught us about them and how they live. We know their thoughts and dreams.

We can be the gods the humans need and deserve. We've been with them; we can be better. You're the god of chaos, if you're worried about history repeating itself, be chaotic."

Set stared at Athena, stunned. His face shifted his emotions changed from surprise, to anger to sadness to finally acceptance.

"All right," he said. "I trust you, Athena. Your wisdom has yet to fail, and I'm banking on that."

"So, you're agreeing?" Lucifer asked, clearly impatient.

Set nodded.

"Perfect," Lucifer said. "We can get this show on the road. War, you have the floor."

Lucifer moved to the side while War moved forward. The way War approached interested Athena. He didn't walk or float, instead the ground shifted under him. War gazed out over the assembled gods.

"You know who I am and what I'm about. My task is a very simple matter. I require three volunteers, one from each pantheon. These three will don their weapons and armour and fight to the death. The victor will live and you will be one quarter closer to achieving your weapons."

"A fight to the death?" Thoth asked. "Doesn't that mean that we'll be down fighters once we get our weapons?"

"Once you have your weapons, numbers won't matter for you. You'll be more than strong enough to take on the battle ahead. So, who volunteers? Or do I have to pick?"

Ares raised his sword.

"For Olympus, I, Ares, son of Zeus, will fight."

"A grand choice, war god," War said.

Tyr stepped forward

"For Asgard, I, Tyr, will fight."

"It will be an honour to see you fight," War replied.

The Egyptians all looked at each other, unsure as to who should step forward. Finally, Nephthys stepped forward.

"I, Nephthys of Egypt, agree to fight, and to die."

"Show those men what a woman can do," War said.

Nephthys grinned as she stepped into the centre of the arena with Ares and Tyr. Armour and weapons formed around their bodies, dressing them in the style of battle garb and weapons they were most familiar with. Ares held his spear over his shield, ready for a fight. His sword remained at his hip. Tyr readied his shield and sword while Nephthys held a khopesh, a single bladed sword with a hook on the other end.

War walked toward the gods.

"Warriors, only one may survive. Fight hard, fight strong and fight wise. Your victory will not be an easy one. Now, fight!"

Ares planted his feet as Tyr and Nephthys lunged toward him. They'd seen him as the clear winner and had chosen to eliminate the one who would be able to kill them easily. Both attacks bounced off Ares's shield as he jabbed his spear in Tyr's direction, catching him in the thigh. The wound hadn't been much more than a scratch, but Tyr grunted with pain.

Athena reached to the warriors with her mind to feel the pain but found herself blocked off. War filled her head. He looked over to her, his disapproving stare telling her to back off and let the fight be won by the most worthy.

Tyr slashed down on Ares's shield, sending a small sliver of bronze flying. Nephthys took her khopesh, hooking the top of Ares's shield, opening his face for an attack. Ares dropped his spear immediately and in the blink of an eye, had his sword in hand.

As Nephthys pulled, Ares jabbed his sword into her face, catching her between the eyes. Nephthys screamed as her blood poured from her face and down her body. Ares pulled his sword from her face and threw his shield at Tyr, knocking him off balance. Ares dipped and grabbed the khopesh Nephthys dropped. He hooked the back of her neck and pulled her into his blade.

"You deserved a quick death. I'm sorry you suffered."

Blood poured from her mouth until she finally fell to the ground. Ares turned and stared at Tyr, and Athena took a step back when she caught the cold calm within his eyes. The man Tyr was about to fight wasn't the chaotic warrior she'd always known. Ares was clearly studying his opponent, learning his moves and finding ways to counter them.

Ares' expression told Athena he'd had enough of fighting and wanted nothing more than for the bloodshed to end. The only way for him to accomplish such a task would be to win the fight, get the weapons, and kill the angels.

Athena shook her head; she shouldn't have been able to read him so well. War must have let her in for a moment.

"Tyr," Ares said, his voice low and calm, "I've always respected you as a fighter and a warrior. I just wanted you to know that."

"Your respect honours me," Tyr said "I accept my death at your hand, but don't expect it to be easy."

Ares grinned. "I'd lose respect if you made it easy."

Tyr spun his sword and readied his shield. Ares tightened his grip on his sword and the khopesh. The two paced in a circular motion, keeping the distance between them as wide as possible. Ares lunged, both weapons ready for attack. Tyr knocked the khopesh out of the way with his shield while deflecting Ares's sword. Ares dipped and slashed the khopesh's edge along Tyr's underarm.

Tyr forced his shield down into Ares's helmet, knocking Ares to the ground. Tyr stood over Ares, ready to take the final blow.

"You came in too fast Ares," Tyr said.

"That's where you're wrong."

Ares took his sword and stabbed the end into Tyr's foot. In a flash, the sword moved upward, removing Tyr's other hand. Tyr screamed as his hand and sword fell to the ground beside Ares. The God of War stood and shook his head. "You're a great fighter. This is such a waste."

Tyr nodded and raised his head, giving Ares a clear shot at his neck. Ares pressed his lips together as he swung his sword. Tyr's head came cleanly away from his body and fell to the ground with a sickening crunch.

"Your victor, the Olympian, Ares!" War declared.

Nobody cheered. They gave Ares acknowledgement as the victor as he walked back to the rest of the gods. Athena placed her hand on her brother's shoulder and gave him a nod of acceptance.

"You okay?" she asked.

"I'm done with fighting," he said.

Athena closed her eyes for a moment. When she opened them, she said, "I know."

Lucifer stepped forward. "War has been appeased. He has informed me that Ares is accepted to enter the underworld with me."

War nodded before melting back into his shapeless form and dissolving away into nothing, leaving three Horsemen behind.

"Now," Lucifer continued, "We have someone of great importance in our midst. I would like to introduce someone who has done a lot of work these past few days and has been enjoying his job creating new and incredible super viruses and bacteria. The one, the only, Pestilence!"

The white shapeless form on the right turned a sickly yellow colour and flew to the ground in the centre of the arena. Like War, Pestilence began to take a human form. He was unnaturally thin, his bones visible through his skin. Black patchy hair made his skin look even more jaundiced than before. He wore a loose-fitting t-shirt and sweatpants tied tight to his belt. The face Pestilence wore showed sunken eyes, a hooked nose and sharp cheekbones. If he had been human, he would have been considered a terminal patient.

"Greetings gods," Pestilence said, his voice hardly more than an audible whisper. The gods heard him in their heads more than his actual spoken voice. "I have a demand for you all. This will not require any of you to be missing from the fight, nor will it require any of you to die. I only have a simple favour. I need a plague-rat to be set free in the Middle East. I have a new virus that I've been developing, and it requires a trial run."

Hermes raised his hand and asked, "Why the Middle East?"

Pestilence scowled. "Why not the Middle East? What business is it of yours?"

"Curiosity?" Hermes replied.

"Fine. I'll enlighten you. North America has too many resources.

My plague would be over before it begins. If I infected Asia, it would destroy the species. There are just too many people and they go everywhere. It would get out of hand. And, I'm tired of shitting all over Africa. They've suffered enough and deserve a break from all the diseases.

"The Middle East has a good healthcare system, but my plague would have a chance to actually spread and provide me with the data I need. The god who takes on this task will be there, infecting people for a full year. They will show no symptoms, nor will anyone suspect them as a carrier. They would be my perfect plague-rat."

Apophis raised his hand. "I will happily take this task."

"Not you. It must be a sacrifice from one of you. It must be a god or goddess of healing. Many of you hold several categories, some of which you're not as well-known for. Artemis, I choose you to be my plague-rat. Do you accept this role?"

Artemis looked to the other gods, looking for someone to speak up for her in defence. "You want me?' she asked. "I'm a goddess of the hunt."

Pestilence grinned, and for the first time Athena could see there wasn't a tooth in his mouth.

"You carry many titles, Artemis; the goddess of the hunt, the dark, the light, the moon, wild animals, nature, wilderness, childbirth, virginity, fertility, young girls, and health. Don't get me wrong, if I could get Panacea in this role, I would. But she's not here, nor a part of this war. She's doing work in a part of Africa I can't even touch. So, with a lack of options, I choose you."

Artemis looked as if she wanted to fight Pestilence's decision, her face twisted into a snarl.

"No," she said, "I'm not sacrificing my own ideals for this. I'll happily die; I'll happily let us all die if it means not killing humans. That's exactly what Set was talking about, putting humans at risk for our own gain. I won't do it."

Pestilence nodded, "Very well."

"I'm sorry everyone," Artemis said, "I just can't allow myself to do this. It's not that I'm a god of healing; it's that I'd be no better than the monsters out there currently fighting. None of us would."

"And that's why you pass," Pestilence said. "This virus would have destroyed the planet no matter where you went. You didn't know that, and still you refused to kill humans. I approve."

Pestilence stepped back and morphed back to his shapeless form. He flew around the room and vanished. Lucifer shook his head.

"A cheap trick. I wonder what he would have done if you had agreed. I guess we'll never know. Anyway, Pestilence says Thor... for some reason... Thor is permitted to enter Hell. He wasn't even a part of this, but whatever."

Thor's eyes grew wide as he heard where he was going. He sighed through his nose and said, "I accept my responsibility."

"Our next guest is a familiar face in many places around the world," Lucifer continued "Anywhere there has been too much or too little rain, anywhere mites or locusts have swarmed. Next up is Famine!"

Of the two shapeless forms remaining, the left form turned a brilliant shade of purple and shifted forward. Like War and Pestilence before it, Famine began to take human form, shifting into a handsome man with long black hair, combed back. He had a strong chiselled jawline and a perfect nose. A dark purple suit covered a body that didn't look like it hit the gym often but was still fit.

"Pleased to make your acquaintance," Famine said casually.

"Question," Loki said.

"Go ahead," Famine said, his grin malevolent.

"War appeared as a warrior and Pestilence looked like he was on his last legs; their appearances made sense. I don't understand your form."

"This is the form I take here on Earth these days. I'm the head of every grain and cattle board on the planet. I know that won't mean much to most of you. Demeter gets it, though."

The fury in Demeter's eyes would have sent most running.

"You're a monster!"

"Many would say that, yes."

"Get on with it," Demeter said, sneering.

"I actually want you, Demeter."

"Me?"

"Yes. You're a goddess of the harvest, and to my knowledge you're the only harvest deity in this room. So, that said, I have a job for you. There's a particular plot of land in Canada that I want. You, my dear Demeter, are going to release a series of weeds and insects to destroy the crops in the area. The farmer will be forced to go bankrupt and sell his land."

Demeter shook her head. "You'll have to get someone else to do that."

"If it makes you feel any better, he's going to bounce back. He's not going to lose his livelihood for long; he's just going to have to move his operation to a different part of Alberta, up north around Fairview. Oh, and before you start getting ideas that I'm pulling the same stunt as Pestilence, know that I'm not. I'm a man of business and I want results.

"So, Demeter, what's it going to be? Are you going to help me gain this land? Will you force the farmer to move to a different part of his province? As I said, he's not going to be out much. He'll have a tough few years, but he'll be better off for it."

"How do I know you're not lying about the farmer?"

"What purpose would I have to lie? To be honest, your aid is not required. The farmer is going to sell to me one way or another. I'm doing this as a favour to Lucifer. We Horsemen owed him and he's calling it in on you defiant and ungrateful little shits."

Famine's voice rose in frustration. "You should be kissing our fucking feet for even considering helping you. You may think defying us makes a difference, but I have news for you sunshine. Shit, I have news for all of you. We're going to do what we do because that's what we do! War will continue fighting! Pestilence will continue introducing diseases! I will continue to destroy crops and kill animals! Death will continue to do what he does!"

Famine stopped, cleared his throat and straightened his tie. "Now that we have that out of the way, you have my word the farmer will be fine. I have no ill will toward him, and his efforts will be beneficial to me in the long run. So, I'm going to ask you this, one last time. Will you do as I ask?"

Demeter hung her head. "I will."

"Excellent. I will meet with you once your war is over. If you survive, that is."

Famine placed a finger on his forehead, gave the gods a farewell nod and morphed back into his shapeless form. He sank into the floor and was gone.

Lucifer stepped forward once again and addressed the gods.

"Famine tells me that because he must choose an Egyptian deity, he picks Sekhmet. I couldn't tell you why, and he won't tell me his reasoning. So, we're just going to move on."

Lucifer paused for a moment, his face nervous as he thought of the remaining Horseman. "Now, I have one very simple thing to say before we get to our final Horseman. Do not piss this guy off. Seriously, don't do it. If he wants something, and he most assuredly will, do it. Somebody better fucking volunteer faster than any of you other fuckers have so far. This being is the only thing in all of creation that scares the fuck out of me. He could end us all with a thought. So," Lucifer ended with a sigh, "without any further ado, may I present Death."

The final shapeless form turned black as it moved to the centre of the arena. Athena couldn't imagine what death would become: a hooded skeleton as per cultural depiction? A man in a suit like a funeral worker? A crazed psychopath? The options seemed endless.

To her surprise, Death's form was none of these. He shifted and morphed into an infant, only weeks old.

"Thank you, Lucifer, that was very sweet of you to warn the gods about me. But that really wasn't necessary. If they don't do as I ask, they just won't get the weapons. I don't think I need to threaten them any farther than that. As far as you and I go though, Lucifer, I don't like you, and you know that. But, you traded in your only favour for them, and I respect that. Take that as comfort. I may not like you, but you have my respect."

Lucifer bowed. "Thank you Death."

"All right," Death said. "I assume some of you may be wondering about my form. After all, you had the same question for Famine and all he did was have a set of clothes that didn't make sense to you. I am the oldest being in this universe. I am tied to it irrevocably for my own life span. I age as the universe ages. This universe, though fourteen billion years old, is still in its infancy. When this universe dies, I will join it in its silence.

"I am Death, neither good nor evil. I am a part of all life, including your own. This war is not the first war of gods, nor will it be the last. There will be deity battles long after the human race and all other life becomes extinct.

"If I could, I'd allow you into Hell without a demand. A death here is pointless and gets none of us anywhere. But old magic dictates that the ritual requires a demand. For my demand, one of you must die. I don't care who, but I must take your life. Who is it going to be?"

"I'll go," Khonshu said when Death had finished talking.

"Khonshu?" Hathor said, her voice quivering.

"I'm not a warrior," he said. "I've been thinking since Death started talking, and I came to a conclusion. I can't fight, and if I try, I'll get in the way. If I can do this one thing to help, I'll do it."

"An honourable sacrifice," Death said. "Moon God, you will be treated well in your afterlife."

Khonshu's eyes widened. "There's an afterlife for gods?"

"Not usually, but you will get one."

Khonshu bowed his head and approached the infant.

"What do I need to do?' he asked.

Death reached out. "Just take my hand."

Khonshu knelt and took Death's hand. In an instant the moon god's body went slack and fell to the floor.

"It is done," Death said. "I take no pleasure in this, and I hope you do not allow his death to be in vain. I hope you don't allow any of the deaths to be in vain.

"Sif," Death said, "congratulations on your pregnancy. It will be a boy and he will live to be three thousand, nine hundred and eighty-five."

"A short life for a god," Sif said.

"Indeed," Death agreed, "but there are some things even I cannot change. In any case, he will be a beacon of hope for many of the humans across the land, as well as a brave warrior."

Death began to fade away, not shifting back to his shapeless form.

"That is," Death continued, his body fully gone, "If he survives the war."

Without another word, Death was gone, taking the bodies of the fallen with him. Lucifer waited several seconds before walking back to the centre of the arena, ensuring Death as well as the other Horsemen had truly gone.

"Death has opened the way," he said. "Ares, Thor, Sekhmet, hold onto me as we phase. Whatever you do, do not let go. You don't want to be lost within the nothing between."

Athena watched as Lucifer, Ares, Thor and Sekhmet vanished in a burst of flame, leaving a smell of sulphur behind. She turned as she herself was transported through Hellfire and wound up in her apartment.

She looked around, seeing her kitchen around her. A note on her refrigerator said:

Stay here; you'll know when to leave.

Lucifer

Athena looked around for any other sign or message before sitting down on her couch. She waited patiently for whatever sign Lucifer had planned. She suspected it would likely be the return of her weapons.

Chapter 8

Ares opened his eyes to the hellscape before him. Large pillars of grey stone in the distance stood wreathed in flame. To his left rose a cliff of scorched granite, reaching upward toward a deep purple sky. To his right was another cliff overlooking what he believed to be most Hell. Flames and lava illuminated the landscape, leaving nothing in shadows.

Screams of agony mingled with the moans of anguish and cackles of insanity. Ares could feel his heart pounding in his chest. He'd never been to the underworld before; he wondered if this was what Hades saw every day.

"Sorry about the mess," Lucifer said. "I didn't really have the opportunity to clean up."

"This . . . this place," Sekhmet stammered.

"What's wrong?' Lucifer asked.

"This place," Thor said. "It's horrific."

"Gee, I'm sorry. I thought two war gods and a warrior would have been able to handle the suffering of others. I could have sworn they could have handled the smell of blood and the sounds of pain. I guess I was wrong."

"Not like this," Ares said. "There's a victor with war. There's triumph and glory."

"You mean to tell me you've never seen a pyrrhic victory? Yeah, there's a victor, but at a substantial loss and more pain and suffering than necessary."

"War is different," Sekhmet said, making it clear that her words were the end of the discussion.

The gods snarled as Lucifer shrugged indifferently.

"What part of Hell is this?" Ares asked, "Is this the majority of it?"

Lucifer turned to Ares and grinned.

"Oh buddy, this is only a fraction of Hell. This is where people who kill themselves go. Once they get here, we show them on repeat the pain they caused all their loved ones. After that, we show them illusions of their loved ones doing what they did to themselves. Give them a taste of what they did to those they cared about. After that, they must go through their suicide over and over, only much more slowly."

"That's horrible," Sekhmet whimpered.

"It's Hell, what did you expect?" Lucifer said. "Thankfully, most don't stay more than a year before transferring to The Field. So, take solace in that their punishment isn't long. After all, they've suffered enough. Most people in the rest of Hell stay way longer than a year. Most are here for decades before finally being able to transfer. Actually, there are probably still a few from the Crusades here."

"If you don't mind," Ares cut in, "we should get going. Our people are dying out there, and we really don't have a lot of time."

"Are you sure?" Lucifer asked. "I could give you a guided tour through Hell. It won't take long if we fly."

"Yeah, I mind. We have too much to do for a long voyage through Hell."

"Very well, I'll give the tour to someone who actually wants to see the intricacies of Hell and how we run things here. Maybe that immortal woman would be interested."

"Good, let's go."

"Hold up there, Zippy," Lucifer said. "You're not going to be able to find your way through Hell so easily without me, and if I'm taking you, you're going to do as I say. Capiche?"

"When you're ready, then."

Lucifer stared out to the suicide wasteland and sighed.

"It always saddens me to be here. It's not because I have to prolong the suffering they feel, it's because of all the wasted opportunity represented here. If a few of these people held on a little longer, their happiness would likely have been realized. They could have made a real difference in the world. But they let hardship weigh them down. Some of them didn't even really have it all that bad; they just saw it that way."

Lucifer shook his head. "I better get you guys going. We have a long way to go and several other areas that we need to fly through before we can get to your chest.

"I do have to warn you, what you're about to see will haunt you in ways you may not realize. I scolded you before, but this is a very real place with very real atrocities happening to souls that deserve it. Nobody is here by accident, and they receive punishments based on their crimes in life. The purpose of Hell is to help souls atone for their sins, sometimes, or many times I should say, and the results are not exactly pleasant to look at."

Ares, Thor and Sekhmet nodded in agreement before Lucifer closed his eyes and sprouted a set of twelve-foot, pure white, magnificent feathered wings. Lucifer began to grow, his wings with him. The gods watched in amazement as Lucifer continued to stretch upward until he stood nearly twenty feet tall.

"Hop on my back," he said, kneeling, "Do not touch the wings, do not let go and most importantly, do not get drawn in by the scenes around you. I seriously cannot stress that enough."

"What do you mean by letting ourselves get drawn in?" Thor asked.

"What the fuck does it sound like?" Lucifer snapped. "Don't get drawn in. Try not to lose yourselves to the suffering. Proxy pain is real here, and it's dangerous. Where we have to go, it's very possible for the uninitiated to lose oneself and get drawn in by the horror show.."

"Wait," Sekhmet said, "didn't you just offer us a full tour of Hell? What could have stopped us from being drawn in by that?"

"I wouldn't have taken you to the places you'll see with a straight flight. You would have gotten the gist of Hell and what it offers, but not the true horrors. At least not until we got to The Pit. The tour could have initiated you to what you'd see and prepare you. You probably would have managed to leave here unharmed if you'd accepted."

"The Pit?" Thor asked.

"That's where we're going," Lucifer replied. "That's where your weapons are. Demons won't even go in The Pit, so you know the weapons are safe."

"What is the Pit? That's what I meant," Thor said.

Lucifer gave him a grave look. His mouth tightened and his eyes widened.

"We'll get there. It's best if I explain it then."

"Is it too late to accept the tour?" Sekhmet asked, already knowing the answer.

Ares jumped on Lucifer's back, grabbing his right shoulder. Sekhmet was the next to jump up, grabbing the left shoulder. Thor climbed up and wrapped his arms around Lucifer's neck.

"This going to be okay?" Thor asked, "I don't want to cut off your air."

"I don't need air," Lucifer said. "The throat is purely aesthetic. Just get yourself comfortable and secure and we can be off."

The gods positioned themselves so they wouldn't fall and waited for Lucifer to take flight.

"Hold on," Lucifer said.

He stood and broke into a run toward the cliff overlooking the suicide valley. His movements were fluid and smooth, as he took care not to jostle the gods trying to hang on to his finely-crafted shoulders and throat.

At the edge of the cliff, Lucifer launched himself from the ledge, opened his gargantuan wings and took flight. Ares could feel his body being pulled toward Lucifer's; he couldn't be sure if the pull had been caused by the updraft from Lucifer's wings or some magic the archangel manifested.

Ares closed his eyes, doing his best to not look down at the souls who were undoubtedly going through greater torment than what life could have ever given them. He knew the souls were where they were for a reason, but he didn't need to see it.

"Now leaving suicide valley," Lucifer said. "We are now entering where the murderers go."

Ares opened his eyes. He didn't want to but couldn't seem to help himself. He couldn't see much beyond the dense black smoke floating above whatever cruel tortures were going on beneath them, though Ares could imagine it.

Lucifer's wings began to dissipate the smoke, revealing thousands of souls. Ares could see many with knives jutting from their flesh, being stabbed repeatedly by floating blades. One clawed at his neck, trying to fight off an invisible, intangible strangler.

Lucifer dove into the area, giving the gods a better look. The scent of blood and sweat washed over Ares and filled his nose. He swallowed the urge to sneeze while he grimaced at the carnage below him. He looked over Lucifer's shoulder to see a man attached to a chunk of wood, his entrails strewn around by an unseen enemy.

"That's Jack the Ripper," Lucifer said coldly. "He's a recent addition to our menagerie of souls. I'm actually impressed someone finally got him after all these years."

Ares took another look, despite his mental protests. Jack didn't look like the sort of person he'd have expected. His hair and beard had been trimmed into a modern style; his clothing, or what remained of it, had been fashioned from material suited to a man who recently died. Ares thought to ask how Jack the Ripper managed to live into the twenty-first century but chose to remain silent. It didn't matter anyway.

Lucifer continued his flight as a large stone wall approached.

"We're almost through the murderer area and we're on our way to where we keep the liars and thieves. This is a pretty dull place. That said, thieves tend to be less likely to change their ways so people generally spend a long time there."

They crossed the large grey wall to a flat plane filled with naked people. Both men and women wandered around the flat area, not a stitch on their bodies. They all stood and argued with one another. Ares couldn't understand a single word they shouted; instead he ignored the cacophony around him and kept his eyes fixed on the next wall.

"Hey, I have a question," Sekhmet said. "Mind if I ask?"

"Go for it," Lucifer said.

"Where do the accidents go?"

"Accidents?"

"The stuff that wasn't intended to happen," Sekhmet said. "Like someone goes through an intersection and gets killed by an oncoming vehicle. I wouldn't consider that murder. Or say someone slips on an ice cube and hits their head and dies. I wouldn't say that was suicide. Where do those people go?"

"The person in the car would go to The Fields. Someone died by their hands, so Heaven is not for them. But they can live a comfortable afterlife in The Fields. The person who slips and dies goes wherever they deserve to go. Unforeseen circumstances don't hold any weight after death."

"Does that mean that people who kill to save others don't go to Heaven?"

"That is exactly what it means," Lucifer said. "Unfortunately, that does mean a great number of cops do not go to Heaven. They do go on to be cherished in The Fields, though. In my opinion, Heaven is a little overrated. It's kind of like The Fields but filled with boring people who didn't really do much with their lives, or tried to help everyone else out. The Fields really are for normal people. They've done good things; they've done bad things, but nothing to warrant atonement or worship."

Lucifer banked to the side and flew toward a taller wall.

"Where are we going?" Ares asked.

"We're going to The Pit, like I said. The thing is, because you didn't want to fly around Hell, we have to go a different path one that's a bit more direct, but a little hair-raising."

"That part wasn't made clear!" Thor shouted.

"Too late to change your mind," Lucifer said. "Hang on tight!"

Lucifer flapped his wings and shot upward. Ares's grip on the archangel's shoulder tightened. He could feel himself get pulled toward the ground below. The fall wouldn't kill the God of War; it wouldn't even hurt him. But he didn't want Lucifer to have to turn around to get him, if he even would.

He looked over to Thor and Sekhmet who struggled to hold on as well.

"How tall is this fucking wall?" Ares shouted.

"Just a little farther," Lucifer assured him.

Ares looked up and could see the top of the wall. Lucifer immediately cleared the top and landed.

"Everybody off," he said, voice booming.

Ares, Thor and Sekhmet released their grips as Lucifer shrunk back to his normal size. Ares looked to the stone under his feet. It was made from the same grey granite the rest of Hell appeared to be made of, though something about it seemed off, different in a strange sort of way.

In front of him and the other gods sat a massive hole. Ares looked down to find he couldn't see past the lip of the cavern.

"Welcome to The Pit," Lucifer said. He sighed sorrowfully and scratched the back of his head. "I have to warn you, what you're about to see down there is so much worse than anything you've seen so far in Hell."

"The thieves' area was pretty dull," Thor said. "But worse than the murder or suicide areas?"

"Yes. Souls here are permitted to leave once they atone for their actions. Much of the time it's just for them to feel genuine sorrow for what they've done, and we have them confront the person or people they've wronged. If they receive forgiveness, they are allowed to leave. But there are some souls that never leave. They don't strive to be better; they don't care about the torture or torment and come to embrace their new reality."

"So, a person can become comfortable being stabbed or ripped apart?" Sekhmet asked.

Lucifer shot the gods a look of concern, "You'll see. I honestly can't describe it well enough; it's something you'll have to experience. I don't like that you have to go down there. None of you have the right constitution to go through what's down there."

"Really?" Ares said, offended.

"I don't mean anything by that," Lucifer said. "I just mean, unless you've been a god of the underworld, you really can't imagine what you're about to see."

"You're wishing Hades, Hel and Anubis would have come down instead?"

"No, I wouldn't have allowed them to come down here, even if The Horsemen would have allowed them."

"You're sending some seriously mixed messages here, Lucy," Thor growled.

Lucifer's gave him a grim look.

"First, never call me Lucy again. You wouldn't be the first god to be trapped in Hell for any period of time. Secondly, I don't want them down here because I'm ashamed of what I've let the underworld become."

The gods gave Lucifer looks of confusion, prompting him to elaborate.

"I grew up hearing stories about the Egyptian and Olympian gods. Even when the Asgardians came in, I was seriously impressed.

"When Egypt and Olympus fell, the souls from your respective underworlds flowed into mine. It's been a struggle just to make sure everyone made it to where they needed to go. I managed it too, but then the worst thing an underworld ruler can do happened to me. I stopped caring. Nobody ever came down. All I had for company was demons, and they're not good for conversation, especially those who stay here in Hell. Nobody wanted to be around me. I got this reputation as this evil shit bag and suddenly I was alone. I sort of let the place go into disarray. I couldn't allow the gods of the underworld to see the mess I made. Sure, in the new age I've found a new love for my job, but it's not like I can clean this up quickly."

"That makes sense," Ares said. "I think Underworld gods don't get nearly the respect they deserve."

"They did in Egypt," Sekhmet said, grinning.

"Stop bragging," Ares snapped.

"I'm sure they would have understood," Thor said.

Lucifer shook his head, a tear falling from his eye.

"They're my idols. The last thing I want is to disappoint them."

Ares laughed. "You have apparently never met Hades. Even as a god, that guy was probably the most chill of us all. He just did his job, loved his wife and cared for Cerberus. He was . . . heartbroken when both Cerberus and Persephone died. They couldn't leave the underworld, but also couldn't stay. It's like Osiris."

"The thing is," Thor continued, "the underworld gods were humbler than the rest of us. Every day, day in and day out, they saw what was inevitably going to happen to everything and everyone. Being a god of the underworld is a lonely job. It's not glamorous and the mortals want nothing to do with you, because you remind them that they're going to die.

"What the underworld job is, though, is important. You provide a necessary service that so very few can do."

"I know," Lucifer said. "But we should get you your weapons so you can go kick my brother's ass. How much magic do you guys have?"

Ares, Thor and Sekhmet looked at one another. "We don't have magic, at least not enough for it to really be worth much here in the underworld." (need dialogue tag)

"Shit," Lucifer said. "That means I'm going to have to hold you all up while we descend. The hole is much too small for me to carry you three down there. We'll have to go slowly; I don't think I'd be able to catch us all in time if we do a freefall. It shouldn't take us longer than an hour."

"Is here any way we can do things a little faster?" Ares asked.

"I'm afraid not. Now, on my mark, jump. One . . . two . . . three!"

The gods all jumped in unison with Lucifer. The archangel cast a spell slowing their descent to a crawl. Everything went black as they entered the hole; Ares took in several slow breaths to calm himself. He didn't enjoy the thought of falling in the dark, unable to see the bottom below him.

"So, our chest is at the bottom of this pit?" Sekhmet asked.

"Yes," Lucifer said. "Now, if you don't mind, it takes a lot of concentration to maintain our slow fall. If you could be quiet, I'd really appreciate it."

The gods obeyed, the air rushing past them the only indication they were still falling.

A flash of light greeted the gods, blinding them momentarily. Ares opened his eyes to a series of cages around the hole. Most were tall enough for a person to stand, though many were small enough to only allow a person to sit.

As Ares passed the cages, one caught his eye. Inside, he could see a man sitting at a table. The man was fat, fatter than anyone Ares had ever seen in his life. His green, rotted cheeks fell down his face, creating the effect of jowls. His forehead had grown over his eyes and sat drooping to the bridge of his nose. Any hair the man may have had in life was gone, leaving him bare and naked as he sat on the floor.

Looking down, Ares could see the man's torso had split open, revealing his intestines, stomach, liver, kidneys and the bottom of his lungs. The stomach had fully ruptured, showing the gurgling undigested food, stomach acid and bile within. His legs had fully rotted; green streaks crazed them while his rotted feet lay on the floor a few meters away.

An arm as large as both of Ares's legs reached out to a table filled with food. He grabbed a chunk of meat and brought it to his face. Everything came to a stop as he watched the man take a bite. The sounds of slurping and sizzling grease seemed to echo through Ares's head as liquid fat fell from his mouth, down his chin and to his splayed gut.

The man's stomach bubbled as the meat slid down his esophagus and into the split stomach. Ares could see the chunk settle and sink into the stomach acid, unable to truly digest. Ares's breath slowed as he felt his eyes shift from their usual brown to a deep green, the colour of bile.

Ares looked over to Thor who had his eyes on a room filled with gold. Ares couldn't be sure just how much gold was in the room, but the place was nearly filled to capacity. In the cage, a man was on his hands and knees, his face downward. His eyes were closed, the look of sickness clear on his face.

Suddenly, the man's eyes shot open as gold coins and molten gold poured from the man's mouth. The regurgitated gold fell to the floor, the thin man doing everything he could to keep his treasure from slipping between the bars and falling to the pit below. He gathered as many coins he could to his lap as he vomited more gold onto himself. The smell of seared flesh and molten gold filled The Pit as the man's lips cracked and split. Blood leaked from his mouth, which he wiped away with his arm.

The man began piling the gold around him, stacking coins on top of other coins until the piles reached the roof of his cell. More gold was expelled from his mouth, all over the stacks of coins. Several rolled away toward the edge of the cell. He shrieked and crawled to catch the runaway coins, missing three as the fell from his cell. The man cried in anguish as he watched them fade from view.

As Thor watched the horror, his eyes changed from his typical sky blue to a deep gold colour.

Ares knew Lucifer could see everything the gods could see, although he didn't think the archangel had been slowing the descent while the gods watched what happened around and below them. He wondered if that had been what Lucifer had meant by not allowing themselves to be drawn in.

Sekhmet noticed a young woman sitting in her cell, naked to the world. In her hand she held a knife; she ran the tip of the blade down her hand, splitting the skin as the knife travelled. She placed her hand on a block of wood Sekhmet hadn't seen before and began slicing off her fingers. The knife made a thirsty crunch with every drop.

The woman emitted a loud amused cackle as she saw her fingerless hand. Blood poured from the stumps. She took the knife and placed it on the bridge of her nose. In a single motion, the nose fell to the floor and out of the cell.

She then brought the knife to her navel. She poked herself lightly, sending a trickle of blood from her torso and down her leg. She held the knife steady, not moving until she pushed the knife farther in.

She soon threw the knife aside, putting the fingers of her good hand inside the wound. The sound of flesh tearing as her whole hand entered her body sickened Sekhmet. She watched as the woman's muscles indicated she'd made a fist. The woman proceeded to pull out a piece of her large intestine.

The laughter the woman emitted shook Sekhmet to her core. She'd seen her fair share of blood and carnage in her time. She'd been the cause of it in many cases. But she'd never seen anything so terrifying.

The woman wrapped her intestines around the bars of her cell and began to sway back and forth until she was no longer visible to Sekhmet. Sekhmet's eyes turned from brown to blood red.

The bottom of The Pit was finally in view. As Lucifer had promised, the chest created by the three pantheons lay at the bottom. Lucifer dropped the gods to the ground, knowing they'd land on their feet unhurt.

"I have a question," Sekhmet said.

"No surprise there," Lucifer replied.

Ignoring Lucifer's comment, she asked, "If you can't touch the chest, how did you get it down here?"

"I was wondering when you'd ask that," Lucifer said. "Osiris helped me. My father allowed Osiris an extra few days to help me out before he died. Also, I want to apologise for what you saw back there. I tried to obfuscate as many as I could, but those three got through."

"It's fine," Ares huffed as he approached the chest. "Let's do this."

Thor and Sekhmet joined him on either side. Sekhmet placed her hand on the Eye of Ra. The symbol glowed a brilliant yellow, feeling the presence of its kin.

Thor placed his hand on the symbol of Mjolnir; the symbol glowed a bright blue. Ares looked to the other two before placing his hand on the symbol of a lightning bolt. Orange light emerged from the symbol. Soon the gods, Lucifer and the bottom of The Pit were bathed in a warm white light.

Chapter 9

Athena had waited in her apartment nearly six hours before she flipped on the news to pass the time. She watched the night anchors, Gregory Thiessen and Karen Toews, introduce themselves. Athena always liked Gregory; he was a gentle man with a kind voice and a demeanor to match. He'd been there for her when she'd first started with Red City News and helped her carve her path to an anchor position.

Karen, on the other hand, was a bit of a bitch as far as Athena was concerned. Not the sort of person she really spent a lot of time thinking about, but not a nice person at the best of times. Karen had always been much more competitive than the rest of her colleagues. Though Karen had never gone so far as to sabotage another's chance at a position, she did wield the power of office manipulation and knew how to use it.

Athena focused on the screen. The look on Gregory's face changed from ?? to grave as the camera focused on him. The gravity aged him by five years.

"In our top story for the night, monsters of mythical origin have been seen around the city wreaking havoc. It's believed they may have been sent by some unknown force to fight what appear to be angels. While no human casualties have been reported yet, it is difficult to tell how far these creatures are willing to go.

"Heroes from Ares Corp., as well as several independent supers, have been dispatched to capture the creatures and place them in an area where they cannot harm anyone or anything in the city. The Council of Supernatural Beings has also been contacted for answers, though at this time we have yet to hear anything back. Sources say these beasts have nothing to do with a supernatural order and are working on the orders of another master. However, that is all speculation.

"Experts are baffled at the presence of such creatures, long believed to be nothing more than myths. If they had existed, it was believed they'd been killed by heroes of a much earlier time. Unfortunately, at this time we don't know much about why the creatures are here or where they came from, or why they're fighting angels. The police are urging people to stay in their homes until the creatures can be dealt with in a humane manner."

Athena turned the television off and sighed. She knew the public would notice the monsters, though she hadn't expected the heroes to be dispatched so quickly. All the monsters had been given orders to not harm humans in any way, and with the delicacy of angels on the table, why would they? The heroes were a bit of an overreaction. Granted, she could understand why they'd deploy superhumans.

Her body suddenly began to tingle. She felt as if her whole body had fallen asleep all at once and circulation had just begun to return. Light erupted from her as she felt her power grow. Her true armour began to form around her body, fitting more to her form than what she'd been wearing for nearly a thousand years.

Her spear grew from her right hand. Once complete, the shaft touched the floor while the tip nearly gouged the ceiling. From her left arm, Athena's greatest weapon took form — the Aegis shield, a large bronze hoplite shield magically imbued with Medusa's head.

She looked down at her body, amazed at the sight of her long-lost armour. She'd believed she'd never see her weapons or armour again. Even when Ares, Thor and Sekhmet entered Hell, she'd had her doubts. To see the deified bronze and leather again filled Athena with emotions she wasn't sure she could name.

Once she'd calmed, Athena prepared herself for battle. She retracted her spear and shield and turned to find Gabriel standing before her. Athena jumped back, startled at the archangel's sudden appearance.

"You here to fight?" she asked, preparing to bring her spear back out.

"No. I didn't want to fight from the start. Michael's war was ill-intentioned, one I've been speaking out about for the past forty years. I've done my best to dissuade my brother from attacking you. But he chose to listen to Raphael, who told him you would do everything in your power to overthrow him. And with a couple of the rules broken, I can understand the paranoia. You gods have been an exceptional thorn in his side. But this is not your fight, Athena."

Athena cocked her head to the side.

"What do you mean?"

"You have a much more important role to play in this fight. You are mighty, but none of you are even close to being able to defeat Michael as he is. He's close to god status. You, however, are not. You may be gods, but you lack the faith of the masses to gain the power needed to do what needs to be done. People see you as myths. The monsters are certainly helping your case, but you need to have your face out there before the fight ends. The only way to do that is to reveal yourselves."

"So, I need to go on the news?"

"Something to that effect," Gabriel said. "I know a guy who will be perfect for the job. If you contact him, you will have a greater chance at victory."

"How much greater?" Athena asked. "I'm one of the better fighters. If they lose me on that battlefield, we could be losing a lot of gods."

"Where you stand right now, if you were to go on that battlefield, you have a twenty-five percent chance of success."

Gabriel looked out the window as if scanning for something,

Athena looked as well, to be sure she wasn't being watched.

"If you do as I say, with the person I say, your chance of victory goes up to seventy-five percent. It's not amazing odds, I know. But you have a much greater chance of succeeding."

"Okay, but that raises another question. Why should I believe you?"

Gabriel lowered her head.

"There's no reason you should. We're supposed to be on different sides. All I have is my word, and the actions I'm about to take. You see, Michael is going to throw the other archangels at you now. He knows you have your weapons and most assuredly will be panicking. The best I can do is ensure one of the seven archangels never gets a chance to harm a deity."

"What are you . . . " Athena began before Gabriel's words struck home. "Are you sure this is what you want?"

Gabriel shook his head, his? body tense.

"I don't want this, not one bit. But this is the way it has to be. With each archangel's death, Michael gets a little weaker. Even with all of us dead, he's still going to be tough, but killable. I need you to do this. I need you to become the gods you always could have been, had my father not gotten in the way."

Athena threw her spear to the ground.

"No, we are going to be the gods the world deserves *because* your father got in the way."

Gabriel smiled.

She approached Athena and pressed her finger to her forehead. She implanted the name and location of the man she'd need to track down into Athena's head.

Athena formed and raised the Aegis, letting some of her power flow through it, activating the gorgon's head within. Gabriel looked down at the shield and stared directly into the its eyes. Athena watched as fear left Gabriel's eyes and sheer serenity passed over her face as she turned to stone.

Athena stared in awe at the archangel, appreciating her sacrifice and vowing not to let it be in vain. She sighed and forced her armour to slide into Gabriel's flesh, leaving only mortal clothing to cover her. She shuffled past Gabriel, giving her a kiss on the cheek. She opened the door to look for the man Gabriel told her to seek out.

"And that's where the story ends," Athena said.

Sam put out his cigarette, staring at the goddess.

"So, what you've needed from me is to get your presence known to the world?"

Athena nodded. "Precisely."

"I'll be honest," Sam said. "I'm not exactly keen on the prospect of being used. Nor am I sure how I'm going to let the whole world know about you within a few hours."

"You planned on using this footage to get rich," Athena scolded him "You were using me for your own gains as well."

"I'm human," Sam shot back. "That's what we do."

An uneasy silence stood between them for a short while. Finally, Sam asked, "Is it okay if I ask you a few questions?"

"I said you could."

Sam removed his feet from the table and placed them on the ground, ensuring the camera still had enough battery.

"People have been wondering about this for a very long time. I know it has nothing to do with your story or the war, but listeners and viewers will take solace knowing this came from someone of divine origin. What is the meaning of life?"

Amusement twitched at the corners of Athena's mouth.

"I should have seen that one coming," she chuckled to herself. "Do you really want to know?"

"I do, yes."

"The meaning of life is, to live."

Sam narrowed his eyes. "That's it? To live?"

Athena nodded. "To live."

"It has to be more than that."

"Why?"

"It's . . . it's too simple. It's too easy of an answer."

"Does it have to be complicated? Life is a very simple thing when you break it down. Sentience, however, that's where complications arise, and sapience brings even more problems with it."

"Then what's the meaning of sentience, or sapience, or both?"

"There isn't one."

"What?"

Athena crossed her arms and leaned back in her chair.

"There is no meaning behind sentience or sapience. I don't get it: you've been talking to a goddess this whole time, she's basically told you that everything you know about ancient religion and mythology is not what you thought it was, and still you ask such questions. Apart from a few individuals in the old days, deities had nothing to do with the creation of humanity, the Earth or the animals. We were created by you. That's why faith in us is so important. The less we have, the weaker we become. If we're forgotten, we fade.

"Luckily, our people wrote our stories in books. Not exactly in the way things happened, but we will be remembered for a very long time. We might not have the faith, but knowledge of us reigns."

"That makes sense, I guess. Still, it just seems too simple to be the real answer."

"Humans are always over-thinking things."

"What are you going to do now?"

Athena shrugged.

"There's still a war going on. Gods are still being killed, so I'm going back into the fight. I'm leaving the broadcast to you. Gabriel said you were the person who would ensure our victory and I believe her. I know I shouldn't. But I do."

"Give them hell. I do have one last question before you go though."

"Go ahead."

"Are you really going to be good deities, as you claim?"

Athena smiled, her face sweet, her eyes gentle.

"We've learned a lot about people during our time among you. I can promise that we will be the best gods this world has ever known."

Sam stood from his chair and turned off his camera.

"Thank you," he said. "I promise, Athena, you can count on me."

"I'm Pleas-"

Athena's word was cut short as an arrow of light shot through her head, the tip exiting through her left eye. Athena's remaining eye widened as her mouth opened. The look on her face portrayed braindead confusion. Seconds passed before the arrow dissolved and she finally closed her eye and fell face first into the table and then onto the floor, her body limp.

Sam dropped to the floor, terror surging through his body, his head spinning from hyperventilating. Once he managed to gain a slight sense of what was going on, he tried to slow his breathing; but it was a wasted effort as an archangel appeared in the room. It looked down at the corpse of Athena as it decomposed at an unnaturally quick rate.

The archangel gave the corpse an undignified huff before turning to Sam. The fires of rage burned behind its eyes.

"Michael?" Sam whispered.

The archangel stopped moving for a moment and grinned.

"It knows my name. Good."

Michael walked toward Sam and grabbed him by the throat.

"N-no, p-please," Sam sputtered.

"You can die knowing my name," Michael sneered.

"Do it," an excited voice behind Michael said. The archangel turned to see what Sam assumed to be Lucifer. The Lord of Hell raised his hands in apology.

"Sorry, don't let me stop you," Lucifer said. Michael huffed at Lucifer before turning back to Sam.

"After all," Lucifer added, "I could use some company in Hell."

Anger surged through Michael's eyes. He threw Sam to the side, contact with the wall sending pain shooting through his ribs. Michael turned to Lucifer and asked, "What are you talking about?"

"I could just use some company that's all. You kill that guy and you'll come and rule Hell with me, as brothers. Wouldn't that be amazing?"

"You think I would be sent to Hell?"

"I know it. Our father might not be around, but his rules still apply. Not much we can do about that. I mean, I'm given a lot of leniency as I willingly took the shit job that nobody else wanted. Okay, I was built to do the shit job nobody wanted, but that's not the point. Basically, I do what I want in Hell and on Earth within reason. You, on the other hand, are still bound by Daddy's rules."

"What rules?"

"Don't tell me you don't know. I know you know; you just don't want to admit it. You can't kill humans; you can't break any of the commandments, stuff like that. Shit, the only reason you can kill gods is because they don't adhere to the Thou Shall Not Kill rule, due to the idolatry clause. Don't tell me you actually needed me to remind you of that shit. Oh right, you were about to kill that guy. I guess you did."

"I could just kill you," Michael began.

"Oh Mikey," Lucifer laughed. "You're so cute when you think you're strong. I'm leagues above you and I'm not even a god. Even if you did manage to get in a lucky hit and kill me, you'd be the one replacing me in Hell. Remember, it's gods that are a part of the clause, not angels or archangels. I'm still an archangel. I wasn't given deity status. I mean, I probably should have by now, but that's not really the point. The fact of the matter is, if you want your little war to amount to anything, you can't harm either of us. Not directly or indirectly."

"You're lying!"

"Am I?" Lucifer asked. "Or are you too fucking blinded by your own sins to realize you're becoming worse than me?"

"What sins?" Michael scoffed.

Lucifer laughed into Michael's face.

"How daft are you? You're guilty of all the sins. Let's see. Wrath is obvious. You lust for power. You're greedy in wanting Heaven and Earth for yourself. You're envious of the gods' powers and abilities. You're a glutton for power. You're guilty of sloth by having everyone but yourself do the fighting, and let's not even get into the list of your prideful moments. Hate to break it to you, Mikey; you're one commandment away from Hell. And, if you come down, you will become a lower being than me. I would hold dominion over you. You don't want that."

Lucifer paused for a moment. "At least, that's my assumption."

Michael scowled. "Has anyone ever told you, you talk too much?"

"You do, every time we meet up. It's been what, fifteen hundred years? Sorry I haven't been going to the family reunions. Not getting invited tends to keep me from wanting to see family."

"What are you talking about?"

"Just talking."

"Trying to distract me?"

"From what?"

"The war."

"If that were the case, I'd say I was doing a pretty piss-poor job of it. "Look, do what you're going to do. Just understand, there are always consequences for your actions. Also, if you meet our father, you'll be able to absorb his power if you kill him."

"Why would you say that? How do you know?"

"I read."

"Kill our father?" Michael scoffed. "Do you really think I'd sink so low?"

"Hard to say. You were about to kill a human. Killing our father isn't much different. I mean, he's a god, so he would fall under the deity killing clause. I'm sure he didn't think that one through fully."

Michael growled and vanished, leaving Lucifer's laughter the only sound in the room. Lucifer sighed in joy as he looked over to Sam.

"You're safe," he said. "The big bad archangel is gone now."

"You're . . ." Sam began, but couldn't quite say it.

"Yes, yes. I'm Lucifer."

Sam had watched the standoff between the two archangels in disbelief. He hadn't been able to muster a sound during the banter.

He didn't dare move lest either one turned their attention toward him.

"So," Lucifer said, "you have a task ahead of you. It is imperative that you complete it. But you're not going to use what Athena gave you."

"I'm not?" Sam asked. "Then what was the point of all that?"

"The point is not for you to know right now," Lucifer snapped. "Just do as I say."

Sam swallowed hard. "What do you need me to do?"

"I've taken the liberty of constructing something that will do a hell of a lot more good than what Athena could do."

Fire shot from Lucifer's hands as a disk and a note took form.

"Once you get the disk playing you must read the note. Here's the thing, though. You have to take the disk to a player I've left at the top of Ares Corp. tower. You shouldn't have much trouble getting there. If you do, just tell them you know what to do to get rid of the monsters in the city. It's going to sound crazy, but the disk will get rid of them."

"And if they don't believe me?"

"They will," Lucifer said. "I've already put everything into motion. You'll meet the right people to do what needs to be done. Anyway, there's no time to waste. You have a long way to go and not much time to get there."

Sam anxiously took the disk and the note. He shoved the paper in his pocket and held the disk delicately between two fingers. He dug through his bag and managed to find a case to protect the disk from scratches. He gazed up at the archangel in charge of the underworld one last time before leaving the building.

He rushed down the stairs toward the main floor. The abandoned lobby was a picturesque horror story. Peeling wallpaper, a sagging ceiling and the pungent smell of rot sent a shiver down Sam's spine when he'd first arrived. He wasn't pleased to have to go through the lobby again but didn't give himself enough time to be frightened by his surroundings as he hurried out the door.

He was greeted by a blast of cold November wind. His car was parked out front, behind Athena's motorcycle. Sam's heart dropped as he thought about how long the bike would sit on the street until the city finally deemed it abandoned and towed it away.

He thought about Athena and everything she told him. There had been some gaps in the story. He wished he'd been able to hear what had happened in Hell and how the gods planned on getting around the whole child-making problem. But she couldn't tell him what she didn't know.

He could see her face in his mind's eye as he opened the door to his car and got in. Her voice echoed through his head as he turned the ignition and put the car into drive. He could feel her touch his hand as he put his foot on the gas and drive away.

He didn't know why he cared as much as he did. Athena was dead; he didn't really owe her anything. He didn't know the other gods, and a life under Michael didn't seem much different than a life under Yahweh. The only difference would be the qualifiers Michael puts in place to go anywhere but Hell. Not going to Hell for minor infractions seemed like the better idea. Sam pressed on.

The streets were empty of traffic; it looked as if people had taken the news to heart and chose to stay indoors. He'd expected to see people running or trying to evacuate the city, though with the lack of any property damage, there really wasn't any need for it. Evacuation just seemed like the logical thing to do.

He turned down 50th Avenue and drove south. He began to wonder why Athena had chosen a place so far in the south end. Ares Corp. hadn't been anywhere near the north side of Red City, but it was far enough from where they'd met that he felt he was going a long way north.

He ran a red light and watched as the sensor flashed his plate. He couldn't have cared less. The future of the human race's afterlife was at stake. What little life he had on Earth was nothing in comparison with where he'd spend the majority of existence. It was then he regretted not asking Athena about reincarnation.

The thought that people could potentially come back as something or someone else intrigued him. That it could be a reality titillated Sam's fancy. He wondered what he'd come back as after he'd died. A car zoomed past him, shaking the fantasy from his head. He narrowed his eyes, trying to focus on the task at hand. He didn't have much farther to drive, though getting to the top of the tower would likely be a trial of its own.

Sam pulled into the parking lot of the Ares Corp. tower and ran to the front door. He wrapped his hands around the handle and pulled, only to hear the telltale click of the lock. Sam swore and kicked the shatterproof glass. He gritted his teeth against the pain in his foot as he walked away. He peered up at the top and wondered how he was to get there.

"What are you doing here?" a voice asked.

Sam turned to see a man clad in black form behind him. The man wore a black mask covering most of his face. The cape behind him flowed freely.

"Holy shit, you're The Night!"

"Yes, I am," the apparition replied. "I'll ask you again, what are you doing here?"

"I need to get to the top of the tower. I have a device that can rid the city of the monsters. I need to get to the roof of the tower and activate it for it to work. I know it sounds crazy, but I have it on very good authority that this will work."

"Whose authority?"

Sam considered the truth, though he figured saying 'the devil told me so' would go over as well as he'd expect; or at least as well as it worked on him.

"God told me so. I know, it sounds crazy, but there are mythological monsters out there fighting angels. This should be the least crazy thing about tonight."

The Night shot a breath of air from his nose.

"The sad thing is, that probably *is* the least crazy thing I've heard in a while. I'll take you up there, but I'll be watching you."

"That's fair. Now please, we don't have a second to lose."

The Night placed his hand on Sam's shoulder. "Brace yourself."

In an instant, Sam's vision went dark and coldness swept over his body. He took in a deep breath of freezing air as he opened his eyes as wide as he could in an attempt to see.

Warm air greeted him with a sudden gust of wind. Sam's sight returned to him, revealing much of Red City from the top of the skyscraper. Awe and terror filled him as he looked over the vast sea of lights. In the distance he could see monsters fighting angels. Sam wondered why he hadn't come across any on his way to the tower.

Sam saw the disk player lying only three feet away. He leapt toward the device and pulled the disk from his pocket. He opened the player and pressed the button to expel the disc tray. He placed the disk in the tray and closed it.

Sam sighed in relief, pulled the note from his pocket and opened the letter. Carefully, he unfolded the letter and read the two words on the page:

Stand up!

Sam did as the letter instructed, puzzled. He didn't expect the gust of wind to catch him at such an odd angle, pushing him back. Sam fought to regain his balance, but lost his footing and found himself falling from the building.

He could hear The Night shout, though his words were lost to the wind. He wondered if The Night would try to catch him. He wasn't sure about the limits of the hero's powers. Faster than he'd expected, he watched the ground approach. He didn't remember landing.

Sam coughed as he stood, amazed at his resilience. He grinned, believing himself indestructible. "Well shit," he said to himself, "I survived. Maybe I'm superhuman material."

"Look behind you," Lucifer said, appearing from thin air.

Sam obeyed, seeing his body splattered on the ground. "Oh."

"Sorry to break it to you," Lucifer said, smirking at his poorly-timed pun. "Sorry, that joke was a little flat."

Sam glared and said, "So what now?"

"That's up to you. I'm giving you something that I don't give many. A choice. First I have one question. Do you believe in the elder gods?"

"I know they exist, yes."

"You know that's not what I'm asking," Lucifer spat.

Sam sighed. "Yes, I believe in them."

"Under normal circumstances, you wouldn't be taken to Hell for idolatry. But I believe you want to help out the gods."

"So, I'd have to go to Hell?"

Lucifer nodded.

"If it makes you feel any better, you'd only be there for a day and a half. The sake that you go there for Idolatry is what's important. Basically, you'll be there for as long as it counts, and then you're good. You'll suffer minimal punishment, a sermon talking about my father for twelve hours. After that, you'll sit in comfort in my palace until you get to leave. I'd say you'll be there maybe seventy-two hours. Tops."

"Can't say no to that."

"Glad to hear it," Lucifer said.

"Hey, why didn't The Night catch me?" Sam asked, "I thought he could do that."

"Any other time he could have. Unfortunately for you, he was a little distracted listening to my speech. Everyone on the planet is hearing it. Shame you won't get the chance; it's probably my best work in a long time."

Sam decided he didn't want to ask what Lucifer was talking about, instead going for a question of his own.

"Also, I forgot to ask Athena, but is reincarnation a thing?"

Lucifer laughed. "Let me tell you, that's a story and a half."

Chapter 10

"Hello everyone, my name is . . .well, my name isn't really important at this time. What you need to know is that I am not human. I am a being of great power, as will become abundantly clear once you all wake up and find that everyone in the world has heard this same broadcast. And since a good number of you tend to ignore or interrupt when spoken to, and I'm looking at you America, just this once you are going to sit down and listen.

"Those of you in motor vehicles have been given the opportunity to stop, to avoid crashing. So, traffic may be a bit of a hassle when you all wake up. If you were just about to leave the house, make note of that. That said, it's the middle of the night. If you're just leaving the house now, you deserve the traffic.

"I'm here to talk to all of you about something really important. Something that has been going on around you for longer than any of you have been alive. It's concerning the gods. Now, I use the term god loosely. Basically, a god is a being people choose to worship or have chosen to worship in the past. I'm sorry to tell you . . . well, I'm not. Facts are facts. But there was no god that created the universe or built humanity. Figured I should pull that Band-Aid off sooner than later. It's all a natural occurrence brought on by a series of events.

"I suppose I should talk about the beginning, just so most of you who think Yahweh or Allah, if you follow such denominations, created everything. In fact, none of you really know how the universe came to be. The big bang theory is a popular one, detailing a great expansion from a singularity. It's a good story and you're not that far off. It did start with something small, almost inconsequential. Our universe started with an idea. And that could probably have been the great expansion, but that's not the point I'm getting at.

"Back, way way way back, or forward, it's really hard to tell when you're dealing with a person's imagination. Best I don't get too deep into it, it's confusing. Anyway, there was a person who wanted to tell stories. And then he did. Boom, our universe popped into being. Every god knows this origin. We were created with it in our minds. Now, I can't say every universe has the same origin; maybe some did start with a god who finely tuned everything in the universe. Maybe there are some universes where the holy texts are right, but not in this one. I'll get to that later.

"Once the universe formed, a god of gods arose. Her name was Salanis. And to those of you out there -- you know who you are -- yes, it is a her. I don't really know the extent of her powers; her reach is far beyond this insignificant ball of rock and water. It's beyond the comprehension of any god here on Earth. Trust me when I say the universe is a much stranger and scarier place than you'd like to experience. But, if I were to narrow things down, she gives form to the gods that people believe in. Without her, there's no us.

"Here on Earth, there are gods, beings of immense power that hold sway over what people can and can't do in life and determine where people go after they die. If I'm being honest, the title of god is reserved strictly for egomaniacs. Or maybe the ego forms after they've been awarded with godhood. I'm technically not a god, so I couldn't say from experience. But shit, Christ was a great guy until he started getting actually worshiped. Now, he's as big of a dick as Michael. Seriously, though, he did his best to point people toward a society of peace and prosperity, at least to what was good for the day. But, as humans, you didn't listen and killed him. You couldn't leave it at that though; no, you had to go and write books about him, implementing. . . no, that's not the right word. . . Attaching? Yeah, attaching your own ideals onto what he thought. You had to start worshiping him. Now he's no better than the archangels.

"Since we're on the topic of Holy Scriptures, let's get into that, shall we? I have to say, I have no idea what it is with you humans, believing what ancient people tell you while completely disregarding anything said to you in the modern era.

"Hell, it's been shown countless times that the words you'd read in those pages have been translated repeatedly. It helped reach a wider audience and convert more followers. But that's not all. Language changes over time, and therefore the holy books would have required updating as well. What you're reading is not the original text, but instead something someone translated and retranslated and translated again, and since some languages don't have direct translations, messages were lost.

"You have all of human knowledge at the tips of your fingers, but because someone wrote something before they actually had reasonable means to explain something, you believe them. Why do you believe them? I know why, and it's the dumbest reason I know. Because tradition.

"Do you know what traditions are? Do you? I'm sure some of you know; hell, some of you might even have a pretty good idea as to why traditions are dumb. For those of you scratching your heads or trying to argue with me, let me break this down for you.

"Hypothetically speaking, let's say there's a tribe, hundreds of years old, maybe older. It's the early eighteen-hundreds; colonialism has started to spread west and has no intention of slowing. Piece by piece, the tribes are wiped out - not completely, but enough that they are powerless to stop the scourge of the conquering nation.

"Two hundred years later, the tribe still exists, but its culture has been whittled down bit by bit over time, coming to adopt aspects of the people who took them over. Now this tribe lives in poverty. The tribe lives in run down homes with dirty water and electricity that works only some of the time, all for the sake of preserving what was once 'their land' because that's the only piece of the past they've got left. They live in an area that most would consider less than ideal. There is only one reason why this tribe continues to live in such poverty. Tradition.

"Some of you might be thinking, 'Well that's not fair. How could tradition possibly be holding them down?' It's quite simple, really. There are cities filled with good houses and building codes. There are small towns with great houses, complete with amenities and everything within walking distance. But the people of this tribe refuse to have anything to do with upgrading their livelihoods. Why? Because they would have to conform to the expectations of the descendants of the colonists who killed their ancestors while believing assimilation would somehow rob them of their culture. Despite the colonialists dragging each and every one of the surviving cultures from the Stone Age and into an era of maturity.

"I'm not saying what was done was good. I'm not saying it was bad, either. It's what conquering nations do. Though I do have to say, shaming people today for what ancestors may or may not have done is low and degrading. You're better than that.

"Where was I? Oh yes, there are individuals who do choose to leave the tribe while continuing to hold onto their beliefs. Which is good; nobody told them they'd have to abandon their gods, just as nobody told them they'd have to abandon their culture and customs. They are more than welcome to practice their faiths while living a comfortable life. But, because they want to maintain their tribal mentality, because they want to hold onto a certain level of their traditions, they deprive themselves and their children of a better life.

"Tradition is what's holding them back, just as tradition is holding so many of you back, as well. Because a simple collection of words and books written in ancient times tells you to hate somebody, you hate them. You don't bother trying to get to know someone. Instead, you judge them based on something superficial. Tradition tells you someone is not to be trusted, and so you don't trust certain people based on superficial observations. You don't get to know the person and judge them on their own personal merits and flaws. Then you use your holy texts and traditions as a shield, claiming you're doing what your texts tell you. The thing is, though, you only follow the parts you want to follow, picking and choosing what works best for you.

"The thing is, your holy books won't help you anymore. Your holy books are powerless and have been for a very long time. People who cause atrocities in the name of Yahweh or any god don't go to Heaven. To be honest, they never have. I'm sure many of you know the Ten Commandments. You know that part about 'Thou Shall not Kill?' Yeah, that goes for everybody. Just because you claim that what you're doing is in the name of your god doesn't mean you're excused in the afterlife. Also, seventy whatever virgins for blowing yourself up and becoming a martyr? Don't make me laugh.

"There's a special place in Hell for people like you. Even committing violent acts of aggression against people in the name of religion will get you sent there. Being a priest, bishop, pope or any sort of supposed religious hierarchy won't protect you if you're an asshole in life. Plain and simple.

"Let's talk about Hell. I think I got the point across about the idiocy of tradition. So many of you are destined for there, and I hate that thought. I genuinely do. You're all misguided, primarily because you allow yourselves to be swayed by people who claim to speak for a deity. I've been around for a very long time and I can say with the utmost certainty that not one person in the history of the human race has had the ability to speak for any god that has ever existed.

"Hell is actually a very easy place to stay out of. It really is. Just do your best to be a good person. It's fine if you get angry at another person, but keep it controlled. It's fine if you commit small indiscretions but keep it in moderation. A few small lies won't get you sent there, but too many will. Be good to animals. If you're going to kill them, do it for food, not trophies. Or, if you're going to trophy hunt, make sure the rest of the animal is feeding someone. Just be sure the animal is killed as quickly and humanely as possible.

"Seriously, Hell is super easy to avoid, but you lot are still so insistent to go there. You all seem to be in this continuous battle to one-up the next person on how much of a total asshole you can be. Stuck in traffic because of road construction? You take it out on the poor flagger just doing their job. Food didn't come to you the way you ordered it? You shout at the server who is just trying to get through the day.

"I can't say it's overly surprising. It's in your nature. You want things to be faster, you want things to be easier, you want things to go your way the first time. It's basically the backbone of production. Is it any excuse to be a total dickbag to others? No. It's who you are, and most of you won't take the steps necessary to better yourselves. I mean, that would take actual effort and you'd have to miss out on something trivial to make such an effort.

"You're dependent on someone else. You don't take responsibility, but instead pass along the blame. You require someone to tell you how to feel about any given situation and if you're feeling down, you look to others for comfort and to boost your own self-worth. It's great to have someone to talk to when you need them, but when it comes down to dependence, that's when a line gets crossed and it becomes pathetic.

"Oh, and let's get into how people treat others they don't agree with. Let's talk politics and the pure venom that will flow between friends, lovers and family members when their politics don't quite align. What happens if people see a little girl standing over a bear she shot with a bow? What do people do? They wish harm and death on the little girl and her family. This is what I'm talking about when it comes to people being assholes to each other. There's no call for it; they just happen to do something you disagree with, and instead of trying to find common ground or trying to find something that connects you, instead of forging a level of understanding and maybe *changing their minds*, you want them to come to harm. You even go so far as to kick them out of your homes and disown them as family, all over politics.

"There will be so many of you going to Hell, and because your sins are so ingrained in who you are, you're going to be there for a long time. And that breaks my heart, purely because it's so preventable.

"I think I should get to the point of this broadcast; I've rambled on long enough. I may have mentioned it before, but Yahweh is missing. Gone, poof. Nobody knows where he went or why he left, all we know is he is gone. He's been gone for fifty years, so it's not like this is new news, but Michael, the archangel, has decided to take it upon himself to be the next ruler of Heaven.

"I can guess what some of you might be thinking. 'Michael, because he is like god, it can't be so bad if he takes over.' To be honest, I can't imagine much, if anything, would change in your day-to-day lives if he does fully take over and achieve deity status. It would be what happens after you die that would change drastically.

"You know how a good number of you want to make it to Heaven? I'm sorry, but Heaven would then be an exclusive club only for angels. No human souls would ever be permitted to enter, no matter how good or charitable a person is. Even worshiping Michael and his angels wouldn't do much to change his mind; he'd send everyone to Hell or to The Fields, provided he keeps The Fields open.

"The biggest change you'll notice will be a mass disappearance of celebrities and people close to you. You see, several of the celebrities you know and see are gods. Hell, not just celebrities, but regular everyday people. There are those you see on the TV, those you see in the store, those you see walking down the street and never notice. They are all gods.

"A long time ago, they were given a bit of an ultimatum by Yahweh to leave their respective pantheons or risk a losing war. Yahweh was a lot more brutal in those days; he was pretty bloodthirsty and strove for power. He really mellowed out over the centuries as he watched the gods interact with humanity and as you grew and evolved.

"You're still a baby species when it comes down to it. Not much more than a blip in the history of the universe, much less the history of the Earth itself. You have the potential to be so much more, and he started to see that a couple hundred years ago.

"Back in the day, damn near everybody went to Hell. Nobody

was good enough, even though they worshiped harder than they do today, and they were not even close to becoming truly enlightened.

"But when he saw what you could accomplish, he decided to let go of the reins and allow people to chart their own courses. In that time, you abolished slavery, made several technological advances and continued to become more and more accepting of everyone around you. Bigotry, despite those who still desperately cling to it, is almost dead. But you've also done some pretty horrific things as well.

"You engaged in two world wars in less than fifty years, and allowed a massive genocide you then had to fight to stop because you let it go too far. And then you people created the worst thing you've ever created, and you used it. Twice! On the same fucking country! I couldn't see Yahweh at the time, I couldn't see what that did to him, but I could sure feel it. The sorrow and agony he felt as he watched millions of innocent lives snuffed out in an instant. Considering he vanished twenty years later, I can imagine that had something to do with it -- not to mention the wars that were waged almost directly after.

"None the less, technology kept going and people progressed. I'm getting off topic again, excuse me.

"The gods of Asgard, Olympus and Egypt decided to take the deal Yahweh presented. Egypt fought back at first, but eventually followed suit after Zeus convinced Ra that fighting was not feasible. He knew the Egyptians would die out if the war continued. To be honest, I'm amazed Ra listened. Not because he's a proud god, not because he's stubborn, not because he's old. I'm amazed Ra listened because the pantheons really had a hate on for each other. Most pantheons that are still established continue to harbour hate for any other gods.

"These gods, despite their differences, and there were a lot of differences, managed to work together and create lives for themselves. I think it was the gods who founded the precious Canadian city known as Red City. Known as Red Deer back in the day, they chose it because they figured it was the sort of name a human would call it, or something like that. I don't know.

"Anyway, these gods, back when they had deity status, were awful to people. But they were also gods of a primitive people. They got away with doing whatever they wanted. Yahweh was no different, so before some of you Christians begin puffing out your chests; just know yours was no different. Yahweh learned to let humanity do its thing and allowed you to grow and flourish scientifically, artistically and overall as a species. The elder gods decided to continue to guide humanity. Along the way, they learned what it was to be human. I remember watching as several of them came to realizations of how awful they were to people. It was a nice sight to see.

"But that's the thing. Yahweh learned as a god. He still doesn't understand what it is to be human. The elder gods, they do. And they need your help.

"To those of you residing in Red City, I'm so sorry, but your home is a battlefield. You're all safe. No god or monster will harm a single hair on a human or animal. They are only there to fight amongst themselves. Now that I think about it, this would be the first time ever where there would be full-scale battle, several divine dead and not one account of human casualties. Well, okay, one, but it was planned from the start by me and Gabriel; the gods had nothing to do with it. Plus, he's doing well down in Hell as a guest of honour.

"I should explain why Red City is the battlefield. This would also explain the superhumans, the number of supernatural creatures who take residence in the city and probably so much more that I can't think of at this moment.

"Red City is a Universal Focal Point. What is a Universal Focal Point? It's a part of the universe where important stuff happens. To put it simply, there are six hundred sixty-six Universal Focal points across the universe. Okay, I don't know how many there are, but I'm sure laughing at all your faces right now.

"No, there is an unknown number of focal points, but each planet that has one has life on it. Granted, not every planet that has life has a Focal Point, so take that as you may.

"Earth, for being a tiny blue dot on a galactic map, has one of these points and it falls directly on Red City. The city was built around the point. Wherever there's a Universal Focal Point, strange shit happens. Typically, a Focal Point will form because some strange and powerful occurrence happened in that exact spot and forced the universe to take notice.

"I don't know what caused it. Nobody does. It's strange how anyone or anything that could know what formed the Universal Focal Point is just gone without a trace. And this is not gone in the way Yahweh is gone and nobody knows where he is. This is a literal erasure from the universe. And that's nifty.

"Michael, in whatever wisdom he absorbed from Yahweh, during Yahweh's infancy decided he wanted to do something similar to what he did. He tried to make a deal with the elder Gods and give them a safe place to live. Only, instead of giving an actual choice, he made something up and chose to go into a wholesale slaughter of the elder gods. Granted, it's not like he actually has to power to do what he said anyway. He must have thought they would have bowed down much more easily than they did, and given past experiences, I'm not really surprised he thought that.

"But the elder gods are proud. And they got sick and tired of being pushed around. I can't say as I blame them. So, the gods decided they were not going to take Michael's deal and fight back. It was a good choice on their part, although granted no choice really could have been considered good in their shoes. Michael would have, as I said, slaughtered any god choosing to take the deal.

"Now, I need you to look at things from their perspective. These are gods that have not had their godly powers, or at the very least very little of them, for over a thousand years. They only have mortal weapons to fight back with. I have to say, they are doing one hell of a job fighting back. Granted, the mortal weapons can't kill an angel, but that's not really important. In their desperation, Zeus, Odin and Ra called on their monsters to join the fight, a decision I can't imagine they made lightly. Not their best move, I'll admit; but desperate times.

"And here we are. You know pretty much everything you need to know about the war at hand and why you as a species are literally the worst. So, be better. To start with, you can all stop worshiping Jesus and Michael. Worship Yahweh all you want; Michael no longer gets his power from him. But it's not them I want to weaken; it's the elder gods that I want powered up. Their power is equal to the number of followers they have and how much you as a people believe in them.

"What happens after this war? Who can say? I can't tell you what the gods will do. I do have it on great authority that they will become the gods you deserve. What that means is up to interpretation, but I'm sure you will get gods who not only will listen, but will have the numbers to actually help you as a species become the best you can be.

"If it were up to me, they'd leave you all to go on with your own devices and I plan to run that past them if they win. But let's get into if they lose. I know I said that you probably won't realize much of a change, but now that I think about it, there's a very good chance that Michael will try to wipe out humanity and start again. He did get a lot of his lessons from Yahweh's early days, as has been made abundantly clear with this tantrum of a war he's waging.

"It's not a guarantee, but it is a possibility. The gods, they wouldn't dream of it. They like you people; I can't imagine why. I really can't. But they do. They want you people to live long and meaningful lives. They want things to go well for you, and as soon as some of their deals they've had to make to win the war have been upheld, I have no doubt in my mind that they will do all they can to give you all prosperous lives .

"I'm not going to tell you that everything will be all right, o that everything will be all peaches and cream under the gods' rule. Their powers will still be limited, and they still will only be able to do so much, but they would do their damndest to ensure you lot live great lives. Shit, they might even try and form an alliance with the other pantheons, something that is unheard of. Those are the kinds of characters we're dealing with when it comes to the gods of Asgard, Olympus and Egypt. We are dealing with genuinely great people who used to be terrible deities, but who make excellent deities once again.

"That's all I wanted to say. When you wake up, everything may be a bit disorienting. You probably won't know who or where you are. I'll leave you with these last words of encouragement. Don't be dicks to one another, be good to animals, love your families and if you can bring yourselves to do it, worship the elder gods. They need you, and you need them.

"Thank you all for your time."

Chapter 11

Lucifer had dumped Sif, Apollo and Bastet on the outskirts of the city nearly half a day after the events of the arena. It had been a while since he'd been so far south in the city. The houses of the Penhold area suburbs were gated in, as many snobbish communities were. A gate connecting to the highway stood open, allowing family vehicles to enter and exit at will.

To the south was Calgary, a city Apollo had little experience with since everything he'd ever needed in the new world had been available in Red City. It dawned on him why Lucifer had put them where he had. Lucifer expected the three of them to run. He could see the importance of the child Sif bore and could feel the importance of his birth. If they ran, there was the possibility the archangels would be too distracted with the others to follow.

Apollo voiced his thought to the others, explaining the reasoning he thought Lucifer would have used.

"Maybe we should go," Bastet said. "We're close enough to Calgary that we could be there before anyone notices we're gone."

Apollo shook his head. "That's not a good idea. I see where you're coming from, but it just won't work."

"Why not?' Sif asked, rubbing her stomach.

Sif's belly had grown substantially since their release from the arena. Her movements had slowed as her body supplied the child with the necessary magic and nutrients.

Apollo looked at his wife, his eyes growing soft.

"The archangels are smart; they'd have eyes everywhere, even down here. When we vanished, I can imagine Michael went nuts trying to find us. It's not going to happen again; I can guarantee that. If we try to run, he'll know and kill us himself."

"What do you propose then?" Bastet asked.

Apollo looked out over the city before the.

"We go back in and find a place to hunker down. If we show we're not a threat, Michael might ignore us for a little while. The time to sweat will be when Sif goes into labour.t"

"Sorry to be an inconvenience," Sif said.

Apollo sighed and took Sif in his arms.

"That's not what I meant. Hon, this child is a miracle, and will mean so much. Not just to us as his parents, but to everyone else as well. Our child is one of the final rules to be broken, and if I'm correct, Lucifer would be trying to break the last deal as we speak. We just need to hold out and wait for the child to be born."

"What about after he's born?" Sif asked, tears running down her cheeks. "What will you do with him after that? The deal will be broken; his use to the war would be over."

Apollo felt as if a blade had gone through his heart. He released Sif and frowned.

"Do you really think me so callous that I'd allow my own son to die? By any hand? Sif, his birth will break a rule, that's important for the role. It wouldn't surprise me if that were the cause of the pregnancy. But do not think for a single second that I would let any harm come to my boy. He's going to be an important god, and I'm going to show him how it's done."

Sif stared at her husband and cleared her eyes. She gave him a slight nod and stood.

"Where to?" she asked, no longer doubting him.

"A church," Apollo said. "You two had the right idea last time. Disguise yourself with Yahweh's power and hide until you're found."

"Lucifer found us pretty quickly," Bastet pointed out.

"Lucifer isn't really an archangel anymore. He may call himself one, but he's been lord of the underworld so long he's basically a deity of his own making. Yahweh's power wouldn't hide you from him. Michael, on the other hand, should be blinded enough by it. For a while, anyway."

The gods all gave each other looks of agreement and took off toward the city. The Penhold area was bound to have a church; they shouldn't have to go too far to find sanctuary.

They'd only just entered the city when Apollo felt a surge of energy rush though him. He could feel his muscles tighten, his heart pound more heavily than it had in eons and his focus become clearer. Armour began to form around him as a sword emerged from the palm of his hand.

He looked at Sif, who appeared to be going through a similar ordeal. Armour didn't form around her, as it wouldn't have fit due to her pregnancy, but a Norse longsword formed in her hand. She stared in amazement at the blade, gazing at the keen edge as if being reunited with an old friend.

A shrill scream erupted from Bastet. Apollo spun in place to see her body twisting and bubbling into animalistic forms. Her howls of pain were sure to call down angels upon them; Apollo raised his sword, ready to attack while Bastet's change took her.

Fur sprouted from every inch of her body as she shrunk. In a matter of minutes, she'd fully transformed into a cat. The feline looked up to the gods and effortlessly shifted back to Bastet's human form. Her breathing was heavy, her eyes wide.

"Fuck me," she gasped. "I didn't think getting my shifts back would hurt that fucking much."

"Are you okay?" Sif asked, rushing to her friend's side.

Bastet nodded, tears present on her ebony flesh.

"Yeah, I'm all right," she said with a pained sigh. "Just a major shock to the body. I'm seriously wondering why we chose animal forms along with our human ones."

Apollo's thought of the other Egyptians going through the same ordeal. He wondered how many of them had been fighting angels before their changes incapacitated them, leaving them vulnerable. He stole a glance at Bastet, who had managed to stand back up on her shaky legs and decided to not voice his thought.

An hour later, the sun had fully set. They had waited for Bastet's strength to return, as Apollo impatiently paced back and forth. Another burst of energy hit the trio. Bastet, who had been sitting to reserve her strength, jumped to her feet.

"Just what I needed," she said with a wide toothy grin.

"What do you think brought that on?" Sif asked.

"The fifth rule has been broken. Someone who worships an old god went to Hell."

"That means..."

"Our son is the last rule," Apollo said. "We need to get you to a church. You will be giving birth soon. You have our son, we kill the archangels, and we go somewhere to raise our child in peace."

Sif smiled. "I like that plan. I love you."

Apollo leaned in close and gave Sif a kiss on her lips. "I love you too."

"If you two are quite finished," Bastet chided, "we need to get to safety."

Apollo nodded and led the way into the suburbs. As they crossed through the gates, Apollo took note that nobody had been there to man the booth. The monsters fighting the angels may have scared most or all the populace into hiding.

A few blocks into the suburbs they found a small wooden church. Apollo reached for the door as Lucifer's voice suddenly filled their heads.

Apollo opened the door, listening to Lucifer presenting his broadcast. Sif and Bastet followed, rushing to a pew. Apollo closed the door and proceeded to search the church, ensuring no angels were in hiding.

As he roamed around the sanctuary, Lucifer's voice prevented him from concentrating. "How long is he going to keep talking?' Apollo asked himself.

Sif must have heard him.

"I'm not sure, but he's really being mean to the humans. I kind of feel bad for them," she said.

"It's what they need to hear," Apollo said, "true or not."

Bastet joined Apollo on the hunt. Her head morphed from human to feline, and from her fingers grew long sharp claws.

"I never thought I'd see the day when we'd have to resort to using Lucifer's aid."

Apollo had been about to retort before remembering they had needed him for two of the rules. The thought of accepting Lucifer hadn't been one Apollo particularly enjoyed. The gods had always avoided the dark archangel, even when they were still full gods. However, the gods always had a tendency of avoiding anyone in the underworld. For a moment he felt bad for Hades and the excellent job he'd done while a god.

"Lucifer doesn't seem that bad. He wants to help, and I think that's what's important."

"Maybe," Bastet said, "but he is a traitor to his family. I don't know how much I can trust someone who does that."

"We'll cross that bridge if we survive."

Bastet shot him a look though remained silent. Once the two of them declared the church safe, they rejoined Sif in her pew.

"No angels?' she asked.

"Not a one, Apollo said, reassuringly.

He wrapped his arms around Sif as she rested her head on his chest. Apollo retracted his armour to become a more comfortable headrest. He stared forward at the large wooden crucifix at the head of the room. A carved form of Jesus Christ hung from the cross, his visage of serenity and anguish displaying what the real Christ must have felt.

Apollo allowed his mind to wander, his brain plucking thoughts from the air. The most prominent thought focused on the absurdity of the Christian symbol. Their martyr had been tortured and nailed to a torture device. Apollo clearly remembered the Romans using crucifixion. It had been a horrendous form of death, with some people taking days to die as they hung nailed to a slab of wood. Such a device would have been best forgotten to time. However, the Christians, for some reason, decided to take it as their symbol.

Sif shifted in her seat.

"Do you think we'll be alright?' she asked. "Honestly."

Apollo looked down and kissed Sif on her forehead.

"I don't know. Our people are out there fighting for their lives."

"You want to be out there with them," she muttered.

"I do," Apollo said. "I could be a great asset to the fight. But you need me here. Once labour starts, you're going to attract attention. I can't allow you to get hurt. I won't allow it."

"You know I can fight," Bastet said, raising her head from the next pew.

"I know you can," Apollo said, "but two fighters are better than one. Sif is a great fighter herself, but in her condition, she shouldn't fight."

"You make me sound useless while pregnant," Sif said.

"You're really not," Apollo lied. "You could go toe to toe with any of those angels as well as Bastet and me, even in your condition. But you could hurt the baby in the process."

Sif grunted before closing her eyes. Apollo kissed her again before scanning the room from his seat. He always got a kick out of the Asgardians and Egyptians. They were always so quick to defend themselves if they thought for even a moment they might be slighted. In truth, Olympians were not much better, though Apollo knew only a few would have reacted the same way Sif and Bastet had to his words.

He rolled his head back and closed his eyes. He didn't sleep, but allowed himself to relax, just for a moment. He could feel Sif's breath on his chest through his shirt, warm and steady. One of her hands lay on his lap, still and limp. When the hand squeezed, Apollo's eyes shot open to see Sif's eyes bulging from her head, her mouth agape in a silent scream.

"Sif?' Apollo said, removing himself from under her. "Honey, are you all right?"

Her breathing had quickened, "It's starting," she said, gasping for breath.

"Bastet," Apollo said, his voice commanding. "Watch over her. Help her give birth. I'm going to make sure nobody crashes this party."

"What are you going to do?" Bastet asked.

Apollo summoned his armour and sword.

"I'm going to stand by the door and ensure no angels can enter. I'll see the two of you shortly."

Apollo didn't hear if Sif or Bastet protested. He knew he could have been a great help with the birth. He wasn't a god of children or birthing, but he had seen several of his nieces and nephews being born. He knew what went into a god's birth. Unfortunately,, he was also the best warrior.. He would be needed to ensure their safety. The archangels would have sensed the labour and have sent someone. Not even Yahweh's power could hide them.

Apollo approached the door and sighed. Behind the wood would be an archangel, he was sure of it. Two thin slabs of wood were all that separated them from the angels. Apollo silently wished Athena could have been there with him. She could have devised a strategy to make sure none of them died. Instead, he had only himself.

Thankfully, no angel would ever destroy one brick or plank of a church. They wouldn't dare harm a house of Yahweh; to do so would drastically weaken or even kill them. Apollo thought of locking the door to the church. They wouldn't be able to break the door, effectively keeping them safe and secure until the birth. The thought was good, but the strategy would be foolhardy. Michael had sent several angels to kill and be killed for his war. What would a few more be to get to Sif before she could have the baby? Apollo needed to fight what was out there..

He took a deep breath and opened the door. Raphael stood there, his arms crossed.

"You're all that's coming to fight me?" the archangel asked. "I thought I'd see more of you protecting the baby."

"I thought more would have come to try and kill her," Apollo admitted.

"We'd thought about that," Raphael said, "but, ultimately we decided to just send me. I think my brother is a little too confident in his decisions, but that's not for me to question."

"You don't have to do this," Apollo said, tightening his grip on his sword.

Raphael stretched his wings. "On the contrary, I really do."

"Are you not your own angel?' Apollo asked. "Do you really have to do as your brother commands?"

"For the war, yes," Raphael said. "But killing you? The cat? Your woman? That's going to be nothing but consequence-free fun."

Apollo lowered his chin as a helmet formed.

"Very well then."

He took in a deep breath and exhaled; he planted his feet and prepared for action. He eyed the archangel, ready for whatever attack he might bring on. Raphael placed his palm on his chest and pulled out a long, glowing blue blade.

Apollo's hands began to sweat and terror vibrated down his spine, making his knees quiver. Apollo had seen what a true angel blade could do, having watched the fight with the Egyptians many years ago. In more recent years vampire and demon hunters had managed to get their hands on angel blades and learned their true killing power.

Apollo steeled his nerves and took a single step toward Raphael. The archangel lunged at Apollo, angel blade at the ready. Apollo had experience with such a tactic. He waited for Raphael to swing the angel blade, blocking the blow. His sword switched direction and caught Raphael in the shoulder, nearly cleaving the arm off.

Raphael screamed as pure liquid light dripped from the wound.

"That's interesting blood," Apollo said.

"Blood of the true divine," Raphael spat. "Something you will never know."

Apollo shrugged. "I guess we will just have to see."

Now Apollo lunged, waiting for Raphael's block. He didn't

expect to be able to use the same attack again, though he could try it. Raphael blocked Apollo's attack as expected; Apollo changed the direction of his swing once again. As predicted, Raphael blocked the second attack.

With every block, the angel blade sang. The desire for blood and the soul of a god excited the blade. Despite being weapons of the archangels, the angel blades were not holy weapons. They were dark, vile and vicious pieces of magic that craved death. The more magic or power the victim had, the more the blades wanted them.

Apollo attacked from the side, then the front and the side again. Each attack was blocked by Raphael. He could see the archangel's face twist into a furious sneer.

"Fuck off!" he shouted before spreading his wings and taking off into the air.

Apollo watched the sky; the blackness of night hadn't been a deterrent for the sun god. Had it been daylight, there wouldn't have been anywhere he could have hidden. Even if Raphael had tried to hide within the glare of the sun, it wouldn't have hid the archangel. The night had been Artemis's world. Still, he could see Raphael continuing to fly higher into the air.

Apollo began to think that the only way he'd stand any real chance would be to take Raphael's wings away. Down an arm and without his wings, the archangel wouldn't be able to fight. Sure, he might block a few of Apollo's blows, but not enough to make any difference. Apollo would win the fight and Sif would be safe.

Raphael had begun to descend again, wings folded in, in a dive-bomb manoeuvre. Apollo narrowed his eyes in concentration. He readied his sword and readied his attack. He'd need to swing at the perfect moment, aim at the perfect spot and strike true.

Raphael came at him like a missile. Apollo could see the angel blade, bright and hungry, ready to strike. Apollo readied himself; he didn't care if he died in the fight, provided Raphael died with him. He was prepared for it. He wished he could have seen his son. He would have given anything to see his child. Dying was a good second choice.

Apollo swung his sword and could feel it catch Raphael's flesh as his own suddenly screamed in agony. A wing fell to the ground as well as Raphael's damaged arm. Apollo grinned through the pain. He looked down to see his chest had been cleaved -- not deep enough to hit anything of importance, but deep enough to drop him to a knee.

Tears began to flow from Apollo's eyes as the pain intensified. He'd never seen what happened when an angel blade didn't kill on the first strike. He didn't think it possible to survive a hit with an angel blade. Power surged through him; he stood and forced the wound shut.

"You're too late," Apollo said with a grin. "My child has been born. I can feel him in my soul, I feel the power of fatherhood surging through my veins. And I should also mention, I'm a full god once again."

"Angel blades can still kill gods," Raphael said, grinning.

"Glad to see you're taking this in such good humour," Apollo said.

"That's because you're already dead. You just haven't succumbed to my strike yet."

"What are you -"

Apollo felt the burning sensation erupt through his body. He screamed, falling to the ground. Raphael gave an evil, satisfied laugh.

"Angel blades always kill with one strike. You're just strong enough that a scratch can take a while to kill you." Raphael bent over, putting his face close to Apollo's. "Don't worry, you won't have to suffer through it. Let's go see that pretty wife of yours first."

Apollo tried to ask what Raphael meant, but was silenced when a backhand from the archangel knocked his helmet off, sending it skittering across the ground. He felt pressure around his head as Raphael grabbed him and lifted his limp body.

He carried Apollo to the front doors of the church and watched in horror as the archangel opened the door. Sif sat in her pew, Bastet beside her. Sif's arms cradled her new born baby.

"Sif," Apollo said, nearly inaudible.

She'd seen them enter; his attempts at a call hadn't been much of a warning.

"I didn't think I'd have to kill an actual baby," Raphael said. "But he's a god, and as such, it doesn't count as infanticide."

"You're okay with killing a baby?" Bastet asked, clearly shocked.

"A human baby, no. A deity, very much so. Age doesn't take away what he is."

Apollo looked up at Raphael, waiting for the inevitable. "I love you," he said to Sif before he felt the angel blade enter his skull. He could hear a slight scream in the distance before his head went black.

Raphael threw Apollo's corpse to the floor. He grinned as he approached Bastet and Sif.

"Sif, sit," Bastet ordered. "That asshole isn't going to get me like he did Apollo."

Sif didn't look as if she could hear anything Bastet said. Her eyes were wide, tears falling down her cheeks and onto her child's head.

Her face morphed into a feline shape as her claws grew into six-inch blades. Her eyes scanned Raphael's weaknesses, including a missing arm and a missing wing. She could work with that. Raphael appeared as if he were ready for her.

"What have you got, kitty-kitty?"

Bastet dove at Raphael, ducking under the swing of the angel blade to bury her claws into the flesh of his remaining bicep. She bit down on his elbow and worked her teeth into his tendons. Raphael screamed and wildly tried to stab her.

In retaliation, Bastet sunk her claws into his wrist, forcing him to drop the angel blade. With the primary danger gone, she grinned internally and got to work. Her claws scratched and gouged everything she could reach. Her teeth sunk into the archangel's arm and shoulder, slowly making her way to his throat. The taste of angel blood was rich, flavourful and intoxicating. She'd never tasted anything like it; she needed more.

She bit down on Raphael's jugular and pulled, tearing away flesh, blood and tendons.. Raphael fell to the floor, landing on his knees and then his back. Bastet continued to chew and eat the dead angel. She needed to know what made him so delicious and wondered if it was possible for her to eat the others.

"Bastet?" Sif's voice travelled across the church.

The cat goddess stopped, looked to Sif and the child and shifted back to human form. "Are you okay?" Bastet asked.

"My husband was killed before my eyes and my best friend nearly lost herself to angel blood. I'm doing about as well as can be expected. The real question is, are you okay?"

"I lost myself for a bit, but I'm okay now," Bastet said, her eyes scanning Sif's demeanor, "You're clearly in shock though."

Bastet gazed over to Apollo's rapidly deteriorating corpse. She brought her eyes to Sif and then back to the corpse.

"He fought well," she said.

"He did. His son will grow knowing his father's love."

"Do you have a name?"

Sif nodded. "Elpída."

Bastet smiled. "Hope. I like it."

Chapter 12

Apophis had worried he wouldn't be given the chance of accomplishing the one goal he'd set out for himself once the war began. He'd been a god the masses feared; he'd been a god other gods feared. Over the centuries, he'd found himself neutered, cast aside and left for the vultures. He'd gone soft in his old age. Survival required his evil be toned back.

He looked to his target, feeling the repressed evil flow into his body. He had his full power, he could do anything he dreamed, but first he had someone to kill. He peered down from the top of the apartment complex at Ra. Thousands of years had come and gone, and his chance had finally arrived. Ra was alone, defenceless and ready for devouring.

Apophis's skin grew dark red scales. His eyes expanded as his pupils became vertical slits. His arms began to shrink away while his legs fused together. His face elongated and his teeth became long pointed needles while two large fangs emerged.

Apophis moved slowly and stealthily, careful not to alert Ra to his presence. Surprise would be his best chance to strike. He needed to keep Ra believing the snake god would do anything to help in the war.

He wanted the archangels dead as much as the others, but he

couldn't pass up the opportunity to do what he'd been attempting for eons. Before, Isis had always stopped him from devouring Ra while he slept. With her dead, Ra was open, vulnerable, and too old to fight back.

Throughout the war, Apophis had kept a close eye on Ra. He wanted to be sure no angels harmed the old sun god, for only Apophis could kill the old fuck. He narrowed his serpent eyes and focused on Ra, opening his mouth, ready to strike.

The venom sacks in his face filled, ready to pump on penetration. Anticipation filled him. He'd waited so long, fought so hard, and finally his time had come. Ra turned, staring at the giant snake before him.

"This is how it is," Ra said, accepting his fate.

"Yes," Apophis hissed. "It's nothing personal, just how things are."

In the blink of an eye, Ra was in Apophis's mouth. The snake god could feel his fangs sinking into Ra's flesh, venom pumping into the old body. In moments he'd be dead, and Apophis would finally have eaten the sun. If he were still in ancient Egypt, the sky would be darkening, and fear and panic would have swept over the land as humanity awaited its inevitable demise. Instead, Red City would watch on, indifferent to Ra's demise.

As Apophis swallowed the deceased god, he couldn't help but feel a wave of melancholy pass over him. Ra had fought so hard and for so long, his death should have meant something to the populace. But it meant almost nothing. Apophis hissed and spat as he morphed back to human form.

"You disgust me," a voice behind him said.

Apophis turned to see the archangel Uriel hovering over him.

"I disgust you?" Apophis said. "You disgust me. I could have continued this fight for a millennium and would have if you hadn't killed Isis. Ra would still be alive. This is your doing. It's your fault."

"Are all you elder gods incapable of taking responsibility?" Uriel scoffed. "You ate your own kin. This will not stand!"

Uriel pulled an angel blade from his chest. He stared down

Apophis before flying down to the ground.

"Well?" Apophis said. "Are you going to attack, or what?"

"You think me so foolish? I attack, you'll shift and bite."

"It looks as if you're at an impasse."

"You as well, snake god. You strike, I remove your head. But, neither of us will step away from this fight, so where do we go from here?"

Apophis couldn't hold in his laughter. "Not in the least. I can leave; your fight is your own. You choose to drag me into it, you'll regret it."

Apophis turned. He knew the archangel would take any opening to attack. He could feel the air around disturbed by movement faster than the eye could see, the archangel was about to make his attack. In a flash Apophis shifted his head and neck to his snake form and bit at Uriel.

"You were warned," Apophis said.

He turned back to attack the archangel. Uriel was powerful. It was possible it would take more than one bite to kill him. Venom sacks filled as Apophis shifted fully into serpent form. He could hear Uriel's heart rate increase, though his face showed nothing more than a steely resolve.

"Impressive," Apophis said. "But you don't fool me."

The snake god lunged at the archangel, his fangs sinking into the softness of Uriel's thigh. Before Uriel had a chance to react, Apophis pulled his head away; he didn't need to lose his head on the first strike.

The archangel cursed and glared at Apophis. "That's the only one you're getting," he spat.

"On the contrary, I'll get three more in before you inevitably kill me."

"What are you talking about?" Uriel asked.

"I fulfilled my purpose," Apophis said. "I have no intentions of surviving this fight. However, I'm not going to let you walk away, either."

Uriel looked down to see lines of green venom coursing through the veins of his leg.

"The leg should be losing feeling right about now," Apophis taunted. "Soon, it'll become an encumbrance like you've never felt before."

Uriel's face confirmed Apophis's words. He gripped his blade and lunged at Apophis. The snake god dodged the attack, biting Uriel in the ribs from behind, just under the arm holding the angel blade. Venom pumped from his fangs in less than a second. Apophis pulled away, watching the poison travel through the archangel's body.

"Two more," Apophis said.

"No more!" Uriel shouted.

Apophis attacked and landed another strike on the archangel's buttocks. An embarrassing place to bite, but vulnerable none the less.

Uriel was getting weak; he could no longer stand. The archangel stretched out his wings and flew skyward as Apophis watched, fascinated at his resolve. He hadn't thought it would take so many strikes to kill him.

Apophis knew where to strike next -- the one place that could have killed Uriel with the first bite, though a dangerous area to get near. He eyed the archangel, waiting for him to fly back down. As predicted, the archangel would make one final attempt at fighting. Apophis knew this would be the last strike for both of them, and he was all right with that knowledge.

Apophis shot his head forward straight at Uriel, taking him by surprise. His fangs sunk deep into Uriel's throat as fire erupted through his senses. Apophis felt everything as the angel blade separated head from body. He could feel Uriel's strength finally give out and felt nothing else before the two warriors hit the ground together.

Of the underworld gods, Hel had been the most feared.

"Do you know what really pisses me off?" Hel asked, wiping away a trickle of blood from the corner of her mouth.

The archangel Saraqael stood over her, his angel blade still in its sheath. He hadn't needed it. Hel's blood stained the archangel's knuckles. He stared down at her silently, waiting for her to speak.

"I am a goddess of the underworld. Hades, I love the guy, but he's always been soft. He did his job, but never did anything to really cement his role. He's only gotten softer in his time with the mortals.

"Anubis is another great guy, but he's an embalmer. He doesn't have as much to do with the underworld as you'd think. I, however," Hel said, rising to her feet, "am not the sort who will allow herself to just get kicked around. I'm the queen bitch of the Nordic underworld. I chose who went to Valhalla, I chose who got to go to Fólkvangr and I chose who was sent to Hel."

Saraqael stood still, his face unchanging from the bored indifference it consistently showed.

Fire erupted from Hel's eyes.

"Do you really believe I'm the sort of goddess you can push around? I'm not. Your attacks have been pointless against me; I can feel my power return as you stand there. Now, show me what you really are capable of."

Darkness surrounded the goddess of death; only her burning eyes could be seen. Fire and smoke emerged from the ground, scorching the air around the two beings. Saraqael pulled the angel blade from his chest, and walked into the darkness. Hel screamed as her fury crackled around her. With a single swing of the angel blade, the darkness slowly dissipated. Saraqael exited the darkness holding Hel's head in his hand.

He gave Hel's look of shock an indifferent gaze before throwing her head to the side. The archangel spread his wings and began to fly away. Saraqael didn't get far before a khopesh sliced through his wing. The archangel's eyes bulged from his head in pain as he fell to the ground.

He could hear feet landing near him, a second before he hit the ground. Saraqael looked up to see Sokar standing above him. The god wore his falcon face, the eyes sparking in yellow fury. The khopesh he held glowed with archangel blood.

"So," he said, "Hel was too boring for you? Let's see what I can accomplish."

Sokar attacked, running toward the archangel with his weapon at the ready. Saraqael managed to get to his feet and pull his angel blade out mere moments before Sokar's attack landed, pushing the khopesh in the other direction.

"So, I will get a fight out of you," Sokar said. "Good."

Saraqael watched the deity's movements, carefully measuring every muscle. He calculated the possible reach and attack possibilities. He didn't want to be taken off guard.

Sokar took a step back and held his khopesh before him. He paused for a long, frozen second before speeding toward the archangel. Sokar was much faster than Saraqael anticipated; he felt the bite of the khopesh as it slid between his ribs.

Saraqael brought his hand down to his ribs, sending power through his arm to try and heal the wound as much as he could. It wouldn't be a masterful healing, but enough to prevent blood loss. Sokar didn't give him the chance to channel his power toward the stump of his missing wing, pressing on with the attack.

Saraqael deflected, though it seemed Sokar had anticipated the attack. Spinning the blade, he caught Saraqael in the wrist, successfully removing the archangel's hand from his body.

Saraqael screamed, watching the angel blade fly off, his hand still gripping the hilt. Fear gripped the archangel.

"How?" he stammered.

"Oh, you can talk," Sokar taunted. "Pity you won't get much more of a chance to speak your mind. It's almost funny: you're this big powerful archangel, but after I kill you, nobody will remember who you are. Maybe a few know your name, but the majority don't even see you as a primary archangel."

"You will die screaming!" Saraqael managed to say.

Sokar approached, khopesh at the ready. Saraqael watched as malevolent thoughts went through his head. The khopesh blurred in the air and Saraqael's left leg under the knee vanished from under him, sending him to the ground.

"This really isn't as much fun as I'd hoped it would be," Sokar said. Honestly, you're kind of boring me."

Sokar swung the khopesh and removed the other wing.

"Just kill me already," Saraqael snapped.

The grin Sokar gave the archangel made his blood go cold. It was wicked, filled with hatred and bloodlust.

"Okay," Sokar said. "Okay, I'll put you out of your misery. But not with this. This is a weapon for those who deserve a noble death. No, you get to die by your own hand."

Sokar grabbed the hand still wrapped around the hilt of the angel blade. "This should be a suitable enough death for the likes of you."

Saraqael waited as the angel blade came closer, as Sokar's force embedded the weapon in his chest. Sokar grinned as he moved the blade straight up and down. Pain shot through the archangel's fibre of being before Saraquael's body finally gave up and fell limp. His sight was the last to go, helplessly gazing as the world around him slowly went black.

"It's been too long since I've seen the sea," Poseidon said, holding his side. "I just don't have the power needed to fight."

"Nonsense, you can fight, you just have to get creative," Zeus replied, blood pouring from a gash in his forehead.

They looked up to the archangel Remiel. Her majesty glowed in the darkness of the night; they had never seen an angel so beautiful. Poseidon gripped his trident, ready to defend himself.

"You really think we've got this?"

Zeus grinned. "Fuck, yeah."

Zeus placed his hands together and began to hum a steady note. Poseidon had seen Zeus take this stance before; it would release a devastating attack which could kill nearly anything it touched. However, Zeus's attack would take time to charge. Poseidon knew he had to stall Remiel for time.

Poseidon lowered himself and leapt at the archangel, his trident ready. He threw his weapon, which Remiel blocked with her angel blade.

"Not what I expected," she said. "A god away from his element and a god so old and soft he can't even get his weapon working."

Poseidon summoned his trident back into his hand.

"You think you're so tough!" the sea god shouted. "But look at you, up in the air, too afraid to face us on the ground. Fight us and prove your worth."

Poseidon didn't know what he expected from her. Come down and fight? Fly away in disgust? Instead, she smirked. The smirk soon became a smile and chuckles turned into laughter.

"You'd like that, but I'm not here for honor. I have nothing to prove to you. I have a battle to win and gods to kill. You two are next in line."

Remiel threw her angel blade at Zeus. Poseidon ran to protect his brother, deflecting the blade with his trident. The angel blade shifted by itself and attacked again, only to be redirected a second time.

Poseidon fought the blade, doing everything he could to keep it away from Zeus. It was a clever tactic on Remiel's part to keep the only defender busy while she made her actual attack. Poseidon looked over to see the archangel descend toward his brother. He turned to attack, only for the telekinetically controlled angel blade to pass by him, grazing his forearm.

Poseidon grunted as pain shot through his arm, from his shoulder to the tips of his fingers. He needed to keep an eye on the flying angel blade. Unfortunately, it meant he wouldn't be able to defend Zeus. On top of that, he had to keep the wound from killing him.

Remiel landed, a ball of light forming in her hand.

"Goodbye, Zeus. You were a man worthy of my respect, but your battle prowess seems to be lacking."

"Zeus!" Poseidon cried. "Look out!"

Poseidon turned again to try and catch the angel blade. The blue sword was close to his face, ready to strike. He didn't have the opportunity to deflect, watching as his imminent death approached.

A sword passed by him, knocking the angel blade from its path.

Poseidon and Remiel turned to see Heimdallr walk toward them, his armour glistening in the streetlight. At his side hung Gjallarhorn, the horn to be blown only to indicate a coming apocalypse.

"So," Heimdallr said, his sword returning to his hand. "What have we got going on here? Looks like you can use a hand."

Heimdallr swung his great sword at Remiel, the blade missing her face by centimeters.

"Two against one?" Remiel spat. "I thought you old gods were all about honour on the battlefield."

Poseidon grinned, knocking the angel blade from the air.

"I see two attackers here. One angel and an angel blade. It's two versus two."

Remiel glowered and flew into the air. Heimdallr swung his sword and sliced the angel's foot from her ankle sending glowing blood flowing across the street. The archangel screamed in pain and rage, her body glowing harder.

"Do you really think that will do it?" Remiel shrieked. "I can kill all of you. I wanted to make your deaths clean, but you've left me with little option."

Remiel's glow became intense, nearly blinding Poseidon. He knocked the angel blade away and shouted, "Heimdallr, watch the blade!"

He couldn't be sure just how well the archangel could see through her own light. All he knew was hitting her would be a challenge. He focused on her location and committed it to memory. He closed his eyes and leapt toward her, throwing his trident once again. This time she wouldn't have an angel blade to knock it out of the way. If she could see it and moved, her concentration could be broken and disrupt her attack.

He landed on his feet and heard Remiel screech. Her light had dimmed and returned to her typical glow. The trident stuck in her chest, buried nearly to the ends of the forks. Remiel's eyes were wide, her teeth gritted as she stared down at the weapon in her chest.

She let out a laboured breath before pulling the trident from her body. She continued to stare at it; soon she grinned and threw it to the ground. Poseidon gaped as her wounds healed.

"It's going to take more than that to stop me," Remiel said as she landed on the ground. She held her hand out, calling the angel blade to come to her. "Now I'm pissed. You did this to yourselves."

As she swung her blade, an arc of blue light flashed toward Poseidon. He managed to dodge the attack, the edge of the light slicing his chest halfway through his ribs. He groaned in pain as he fell to the ground.

She approached Heimdallr and swung again, but Heimdallr moved his sword to block the attack. The angel blade passed through the sword, cutting it in half and removing Heimdallr's hand. He screamed in pain, gripping the wound.

"You did this to yourselves," Remiel repeated, preparing to strike Heimdallr down.

The archangel's glare suddenly shifted to an expression of pure pain. A scream erupted from her lungs as blue and orange electricity arched from her body. The scent of fried hair and cooking flesh filled the air. The angel blade fell from her hand and shattered into millions of pieces.

Behind the archangel, Zeus stood with his hands on her back, electricity flowing through his body, amps climbing while the voltage soared. Remiel fell to the ground, smoke drifting from her corpse.

"You better heal yourself," Zeus said to Poseidon. "The fight isn't over. Thank you for the help," he said to Heimdallr. "We'd have died if not for you."

He reached out to Heimdallr and took his hand

"What are you doing?" the Asgardian asked.

"I'm no god of healing, but I can trigger your hand to regrow. I can also stop the poison from the angel blade."

Heimdallr looked at his open wound and shook his head.

"No, I want to keep it like this. It'll be in honour of Tyr, who sacrificed himself to the war. My missing hand will ensure he is never forgotten."

"Very well," said Zeus "I'll just stop the bleeding for you, then."

Electricity arced from Zeus's hand into Heimdallr, sealing the wound. Heimdallr wrapped the wound in a torn piece of the archangel's garb, cursing Remiel's name.

"It's time to go,' he said.

Zeus and Poseidon followed Heimdallr toward what they believed to be their next fight.

Raguel pulled her angel blade from Freyr's ribs. Unsurprisingly, the god of prosperity hadn't put up much of a fight. She could only hope the rest of the gods would be as easy to take down. Very few deities left were fighters. If she played her cards right, Michael and the rest of the archangels would be able to deal with the majority of them, leaving her to pick off those who couldn't fight.

She rolled her shoulders back;, she could feel another god close by. Whoever it was, he or she was weak and not fighter material. She took to the sky, stealthily peering down. Beyond the shrubs and a hedge stood Hermes, the messenger of the Olympians. He looked to be out of place, unsure as to where he should be. Most of all, he appeared frightened of what would inevitably happen to him.

Raguel descended and said "Hermes, it is so nice to meet you. I've heard nothing but great things."

The messenger spun, fear contorting his face.

"Who are you?" he asked, taking a step back.

"I am Raguel, the friend to God."

Hermes swallowed hard. "A friend to all gods?"

"Just to my god."

She took a step forward; Hermes tried to do the same but tripped over his own feet. His eyes began to water as he watched the archangel approach.

"Please, no," he whimpered.

"If it makes you feel any better," Raguel said, "you won't feel a thing. I'll make sure of it."

She raised her angel blade, but a sudden feeling of dread washed over Raguel. She lowered her blade and looked around. She didn't see Hermes scamper away while she was distracted. Raguel turned back to find the messenger gone. She could sense him close by, though he wasn't the pressing concern.

"Come out!" she shouted. "I can feel you nearby. A surprise attack won't do anything against me."

From the distant trees emerged a giant wolf. She'd never seen a beast so large. Towering over her, its teeth looked as if they could tear her apart without trying.

"An archangel," the wolf said. "Let's see if you taste as good as your brethren."

Raguel's heart sank. This was one of the monsters that had been killing and eating the other angels. She doubted it could have killed any of the other archangels, and it wasn't about to happen to her.

Raguel gripped her angel blade and rushed the wolf. Before it knew what hit it, she plunged her blade deep into its throat. She pulled out and jumped away. The wolf's breathing became heavy; saliva fell from the wolf's mouth as its tongue stuck out. It gave her a look of despair before collapsing.

The throat had been the best place to hit, for the beast had been slain. Raguel slowly walked toward the giant wolf. Careful of her movements, she came within touching distance. She reached out her arm to touch the wolf, to see if any sign of life remained; if so, she'd stab it again, in the brain.

She touched the wolf's nose; it was cold to the touch, and wet. The wolf's eyes opened and her hand disappeared into the wolf's maw. Raguel screamed as liquid light poured from her shoulder.

The wolf laughed.

"Okay, that was fucking tasty. Angels are good eating, but archangel, I've never tasted anything as good as you."

Pulling its attention from the appetizer it had eaten, the wolf turned to look into Raguel's eyes.

"You should have done your research, archangel," the wolf laughed, "You might have known to attack me again and again, make sure I was really dead. If you really had done your research, you'd have run the moment I arrived. I am Fenrir, wolf child of Loki, and what was supposed to be the bringer of death to the All Father. Since the All Father wouldn't have been able to kill me, there's no way a little pissant like you could ever have accomplished such a task."

Fenrir looked down on Raguel, its teeth parting in a sinister grin. "Now sit still, or this is going to hurt a lot."

Raguel accepted her fate. She stood tall and proud as she felt the wolf's teeth bury themselves into her stomach, cutting her in half. She could feel her blood draining from her illuminating the inside of the wolf's mouth. Her arm and torso moved to the back of the wolf's mouth, crunching as the teeth rent flesh and bone. Raguel closed her eyes and felt herself die. She was okay with such an end, knowing there were still six other archangels who most assuredly had not yet died and would kill the beast, sooner or later.

Chapter 13

Father Milton Brown hadn't had a crisis of faith since he'd been fifteen. Even then, it had been short lasting and resolved by reading his Bible.

The initial crisis had come after talking to his friend about faith. His friend had revealed that he was an atheist and went on to explain his viewpoint. The problem was, his friend made too much sense.

Father Brown had always seen himself as rational. While he remained a man of faith, he had taken his experience with his friend and turned it into a learning curve. He had never had any experience with an atheist before, but had been told they were morally devoid and reprehensible by nature.

That day, he'd learned that atheists were no different from him,, and made it his mission to accept people of all backgrounds, as they were capable of the same compassion and goodness his friend had been.

Staring across his church, Father Brown sighed. This time had not been like before. Then he had been dealing with a fallible human. The message he'd received, the message everyone received in their heads, such a feat could only have been accomplished by someone of divine origin. He knew it in his very soul, as he knew the words of the speech were true. He could feel it in his heart.

He prayed to God every day, sometimes several times in a day. Asking for guidance or for health for himself or another. This time, he needed a little more. He sat in a pew and addressed his God.

"God," Father Brown said, "I don't know how to ask this. I don't even know if you're even there. If those words are true, you haven't been there my whole life. If I'm being honest, I don't know how to take that.

"You see, the thing is, I've always believed I could feel you. Somehow, for some reason, I knew you were there with me. I believed it with every fibre of my being. But now, I don't know. It's great to have confirmation of your existence, I'm sure the Atheists are having a tough time with the message, and I'll do what I can to help them. But I need to help myself out first. What do I do with what has been spoken? What do I do with that? Where do I go with that? Please, I know I ask a lot. But I just need this one thing. I promise to never ask for anything else; this will be my one favour. Can you do this for me?"

He sighed once again and wiped a tear from his cheek. He knew he wouldn't get an answer. God wasn't there after all.

He stood from the pew and began to walk back toward the altar. It was possible he might find an answer in the good book, or if nothing else, peace and solace within.

The doors opened and a rough looking man in a scraggy jacket and dirty pants walked in.

"Is it okay if I stay here a while?' he asked. "It's kind of scary out there."

Father Brown swallowed his fear and smiled.

"All are welcome in the house of God. Please, my son, take a seat."

The homeless man smiled. "That's very kind of you."

Father Brown watched as the man walked to a centre pew and took a seat. He gazed at the homeless man for a moment before deciding to approach him. He didn't seem to be on drugs of any sort, appearing to be more down on his luck.

"May I sit with you?" Father Brown asked.

The man looked at the priest, confused for a second.

"Yes of course," he finally said. "It'll be nice to actually talk to someone."

Father Brown bowed his head in acceptance and sat.

"May I ask your name?"

"I'm Chris," he said, holding out his hand.

Father Brown didn't hesitate to take Chris's hand and shake it.

"I assume you're here for guidance?"

Chris shook his head. "I'm here to be safe of the monsters. I'm sorry Father, but I'm really not one for sermons."

"I understand," Father Brown said, acceptingly, "though I thought the monsters had been ordered to not harm humans."

"Best not to take the chance," Chris said.

"You don't believe what the voice said?"

"I believe it's best not to take any chances."

Father Brown accepted his reasoning and left it at that. They sat in silence for nearly ten minutes before Chris spoke again.

"Can I ask you a question?"

"Of course, my son."

"Why did you choose to become a priest?"

"Why do you ask?"

"I'm curious."

Father Brown thought for a moment. It was rare for someone to ask him about himself, or why he did what he did. They all just seemed to accept his choice and go from there.

"Well," Father Brown said, "I guess I became a priest to spread the word and love of God and Jesus. When I look at my faith, when I think about God, all I feel is serenity. Pure joy and peace, and I want to spread that to others. I know I can't convert people as well as other priests. I'm not even sure if I've ever converted anybody. But I don't really try to convert people. I just want others to feel happy, and I find that through my faith, it helps even those who don't believe they deserve to feel happy."

"What if I told you that I'm an atheist, and that I don't believe that anybody created me?"

"I'd accept you like a brother."

"Really?"

Father Brown looked toward the crucifix hanging over the altar.

"We all come from different walks of life. I believe and take comfort in my religion, because that's how I was raised. It's who I am and it's what I've come to accept. Others go through their lives the best way they can. Some believe in the gods they were raised with; others reject them. Some come to find god, others remain ignorant toward him and reside in their own cultures.

"The thing is, and I know this is a strange thing for a priest to say, but I could have been wrong. I mean, before the speech confirmed that God actually does exist. He might not be the only one, but he's out there."

Chris shifted in his seat. "You heard that part?"

"That God has been missing for fifty years? Yeah, I caught that little tidbit. That's the part I'm having so much trouble with. I've gone my whole life believing there was a God out there watching over me, caring about me and everyone else in the world. Instead, I find that he's been gone this whole time and I've been alone with my prayers."

"That's what the voice said," Chris said, "but do you believe it?"

"Honestly? I don't know."

Chris placed his hand on Father Brown's shoulder.

"Look, I know what the voice said. But the voice doesn't know everything. God is still around; he's still hearing everyone's prayers. He just isn't in Heaven anymore. The angels don't know where he is and believe him to be gone. But he's not."

Father Brown looked at his visitor with curiosity.

"How do you know this?"

"The same way you've known God was with you this whole time." He placed a hand over his heart. "This is how I know. Because I feel it."

"I thought you were an atheist," Father Brown pointed out.

"Oh, I am," Chris said. "I just don't believe I was created by something higher than me. Lack of evidence and that whole thing."

Father Brown frowned. "You're not making any sense."

"I suppose not. It can be difficult to explain to someone who and what you are. I mean, I really shouldn't be even trying. But this is where we are."

"You're not a homeless man, are you?"

"I guess it depends on how you look at it.. I am homeless; I live on the street and do what I can to survive. But I'm not human, if that's what you mean."

Father Brown stood, fear streaking across his face.

"What are you?"

"Put it together. I'm sure I gave you enough clues."

"I have no idea. This city is full of monsters, superhumans and creatures of the night. How could I possibly guess what you are?"

"You have the clues. I could tell you more, but this is more fun. Besides, it's not like knowing who I am will change the outcome of how this night is going to go."

Father Brown stared helplessly at the ragged man in the pew. He began putting the pieces together; trying to recall every word the man had spoken. To his chagrin, nothing came to him. He couldn't be anything represented by the Supernatural Council; he had been nothing but kind to the priest. A creature would have taken the opportunity to devour him much sooner; . of that he was sure.

Father Brown could feel compassion rise as he sat back down.

"You're right. It doesn't matter what you are. You're alive and here with me. I'm sorry about my outburst and fear; it was unbecoming of a priest."

Chris smiled, his face lighting Father Brown's soul. "Think nothing of it."

"But I am curious," Father Brown said. "I did explain myself to you. Would you return the favour?"

Chris lowered his head.,

"I can't directly tell you, not that you'd believe me anyway. No, you must figure that part out for yourself. But I can give you a glaring hint."

Father Brown raised an eyebrow at the mention of a hint.

"You've known me your whole life, and you've defended me from naysayers and have dedicated your life to me."

Father Brown's eyes opened wide.

"No. You can't be."

Chris bowed his head. "I am."

"God?"

"In the very literal flesh."

"But . . ." Father Brown said before pausing, "but you can't be. You're just a guy playing me. Or maybe you're just some guy who believes himself to be God. You can't be."

"But I am," Chris said. "I really am."

Father Brown's brows furrowed as he stood.

"Leave this place. I will not stand for such mockery of my God. I opened to you how I felt, I admitted my crisis of faith and you choose to mock the very thing that keeps me going? You sir, are horrible and I demand you leave."

Chris rose to his feet. "I told you so. I knew you wouldn't believe me, and with good reason. Before I go though, I'll show you something."

Chris rolled his shoulders and held his arms behind his back. He looked toward the ceiling and began to glow. Father Brown took a step back, shielding his eyes. The light soon died, and in its place stood a man with a great white beard and white robe. His soft blue eyes met Father Brown's as a warm smile spread across God's lips.

"Is this proof enough?" he asked.

Father Brown was frozen in place; he didn't know what to say or do. Only moments ago, he had ordered God himself to leave a church. Priests, pastors and a cabal of religious sects would have killed for such an opportunity. He was amazed he hadn't been smitten down on the spot.

God placed his hand on Father Brown's shoulder.

"Fear not, my child, I will not smite you for indiscretions you didn't know you were committing. In fact, I would never smite anyone for any reason."

Father Brown's mouth remained agape; he was unable to move. God motioned for the priest to sit, and on instinct alone, he obeyed.

"You may speak," God said, taking a seat beside the priest.

"You're him!" Father Brown managed to sputter. "It's really you!"

"It is."

In a flash, all of Father Brown's senses returned to him and he could feel the anger bubbling back.

"Why did you leave? Did you know Michael would do what he's doing? Why are you here? Why me? Did you really hear my prayers?"

God waved his hand and silenced the father.

"I guess I do owe an explanation, and I should explain it to someone.

"Why did I leave? That's a bit of a story. It was seventy years ago. World War Two was coming to a close, and things were starting to look a little better for the world. There was still fighting in the Pacific. It was hard fighting, harder than any mortal should ever be forced to do. Then America dropped the bombs on Japan. I watched in horror at what humanity was willing to do, not to soldiers, but to innocent people. Women, children, animals, everything died in those two explosions. I found myself in a depression afterward.

"My depression lasted for twenty years until Gabriel came to me and suggested I should take some time off, reconnect with the people of the world and do what I could to teach them a better way. I agreed and left Heaven, swearing Gabriel to secrecy.

"This ties into your question about whether or not I knew Michael would wage war on the old gods. I did know. I knew when he'd attack, and I knew what I was going to do when the inevitable came. Before I left, Gabriel and I worked hard to create a plan that not only would stop Michael from succeeding Heaven, but would end him forever. What I needed was the old gods' help.

"The problem, though, was that I couldn't speak to them. I managed to give them a meeting hall for their Gatherings and set my departure for fifty years exactly from their most recent Gathering.

"Not being able to actually relay a plan to the gods was a serious inconvenience. I knew they wouldn't listen to any of my archangels, not that I'd have sent any. The only one I trusted to fulfill my wishes was Gabriel.

"It was he who came up with the plan to warn them. He managed to get his hands-on Morpheus, the spirit of dreams, and convinced him to do what should have been considered impossible. He planted dreams in their heads, which they should have been able to decipher easily enough. But after such a long time on Earth and detached from their powers, they were just not cut out for what Morpheus showed them."

"So now we're here in this predicament," Father Brown muttered.

"Yes," God agreed. "Despite what your book says, I am not infallible, and I don't cause the flow of time or influence actions of others. What happened and what will happen is not of my creation. Well, except for one thing that I have to do tonight."

"Speak with me?"

"No, this isn't what I have to do. This is just a pit stop. It's me trying to explain myself. Deep down, I feel like I have to justify my actions. It's not really a dignified reason, but it's the truth."

"Why did you think the archangels would turn on you?"

"Are you asking why I only trusted Gabriel?" God asked, and Father Brown nodded. "It's because I could see what they were becoming. They'd been divine too long and had grown complacent with being above humanity. They began to see humans as weak and sinful, unable to guide themselves to fulfilling lives while in my service.

"I disagreed with them, insisting they had to make their own way, whether it ended in utopia or total annihilation. Gabriel was with me on the sentiment."

"You shouldn't have left," Father Brown said.

"I had to. I couldn't bear to watch humanity continue to rip itself apart. While in Heaven, I could feel every death, every sliver of pain humanity felt. It was the curse I chose while remaining a god.

Those explosions pained me in ways no human could ever understand. It was as if I felt the bomb go off inside me, but I couldn't die.

"To get away from the pain, I had to leave Heaven. Now, I must let this play out. I'll never return to Heaven; I know that, and I've accepted it for years. But I still miss it. I wish I could see it again, one last time."

Father Brown looked down. He had been so quick to judge the actions of his God, something he had berated himself for not ten minutes prior. He raised his head to meet God's stoic face.

"I'm sorry," he said.

"It's fine. You couldn't possibly understand. I don't blame you for being angry or upset. Any sane man would."

"But why me, God?" Father Brown asked. "I'm sure there are thousands of priests out there asking for your guidance. Why did you choose me?"

"Call me Yahweh," he said. "Do you know I've heard almost every sermon you've given? I've seen a great many sermons over the years, but very few managed to get me to come back over and over again."

"Really?" Father Brown asked, unable to believe what Yahweh was saying.

"You present yourself in a way that pleases me."

Father Brown cocked his head to the side. "Explain?"

"You know how the Bible was written by man?"

"Yes. Though it's supposed to be your Word."

Yahweh sighed.

"None of that is my word. I never had any requirements dictating that people worship me. The archangels are bound by human laws because I decreed it, but I never told any human to write those words down."

"What does this have to do with me?"

"Well, the archangel thing doesn't have anything to do with you. But, through the years, there have been a great many good pastors and priests who have preached some incredible sermons.

They used the power of their words to move people and managed to sway the opinions of others. You see, it was all for the sole purpose of conversion. They wanted people to join their religions and create strongholds of power for their faiths. The way they do that is through the use of the Bible itself, claiming it is my word.

"Thankfully, in the modern day, things have improved. People have grown smarter and many have learned to use their heads and make their own choices about what they believe."

Father Brown gave Yahweh a confused look. "It sounds like you're congratulating atheism."

"That's because I am," Yahweh said. "But that's not really important. Sorry, I'm trying to stall for time here. I'll try to get to my point as quickly as I can.

"There have been some great sermons out there, but they all relied on the use of the Bible. This is something I don't agree with, because the Bible is not my word, just as the forced or coerced conversion of others has nothing to do with me.

"Do you remember when the voice . . . Oh, hell, I might as well be straight up with you, it was Lucifer speaking. Do you remember Lucifer saying there's a place in hell for the pious?"

"Yeah. That part scares me, a lot."

Yahweh waved his hand. "Don't worry about it, you're safe from it. But most other pastors and priests are not."

"Because they use the Bible?"

"No," Yahweh said, "because they use what they believe to be my word to do awful things. They, as I mentioned, forcefully convert others. They discriminate against people based on gender, sexuality, race, religion or whatever they think they should discriminate against others for and claim it all in my name. I don't want that, I never wanted that. But people point to that book and say I decreed that homosexual people are unclean and must die, or that I condone slavery, or that I want everyone to worship me. I never wanted any of that."

"I still don't see what any of this has to do with me," Father Brown said, becoming impatient.

"Of course you don't," Yahweh said, his face softening, "because you don't do any of those things. You don't even really use the Bible for your sermons. You have several copies, but you prefer to let others talk about their experiences with faith. You talk about your own experiences with your faith. You don't use the Bible, because you don't need to. You talk about me as if I were a friend you see every day, as if we have been inseparable your whole life and have all the stories you could tell just from your experiences with me.

"On top of all that, you don't discriminate in any way. I'm almost certain you don't know how to discriminate. You see every person who walks through those doors — black, white, Protestant, Catholic, atheist, Muslim, gay, straight, or transsexual — and accept them as if they were your own family. You genuinely care about others. That's what I like about you, Milton. You're a genuine person who feels his faith deep down to his soul and you're kind to everyone.

"I came here tonight because I wanted to see the one man in this city deserving of my presence. You're the one man who gets it, not because it was written in some book from primitive times but because you truly believe that being the best person you could be was the best way to be a true Christian. Not belittling others, not being a bigot, not trying to get everyone to see things your way. You just acted like a decent human being."

Father Brown stared wide-eyed at Yahweh, unsure what to say. It was a continuing affliction. "I'm humbled," he finally said.

"No, Milton," Yahweh said, "it is I who am humbled by you. I was brash and bigoted in my younger days. I wanted all the power to myself and wouldn't share it with others. I forced other gods out of their homes, being able to create an army of disposable angels on a whim worked really well. But I was wrong to do it. For almost two hundred years, I've wanted nothing more than to give the gods back their homes."

"Why didn't you?"

"I couldn't. The rules set in place had to be broken. They've managed it, to regain their godhood. Good for them, too."

Yahweh turned his face to a wall. Father Brown couldn't quite see what his god had been looking at, if anything at all.

"It's getting late," Yahweh said. "I should get going."

"Wait," Father Brown said. "I just have one more question.

"I know your question but ask away."

Father Brown pursed his lips and sighed heavily. He didn't want to ask the question, but he had to know.

"There are so many awful things happening in the world. People rape and kill; they take what isn't theirs at all sorts of levels. Natural disasters shake the earth and wars scar the very foundation of society, and I just need to know, why do you allow it to happen? Why does everything have to go so wrong all the time? Why don't you do something?"

Yahweh lowered his head; suddenly the deity appeared old and tired.

"It happens because it's natural," Yahweh said. "Disasters are natural occurrences and people do wicked things to each other because it is in their very nature. It's sad, but it's a reality that can't be avoided."

"Why don't you stop it?" Father Brown asked again.

"A lot of people might tell you it's all a part of a greater plan — that I know where every person is going to go in life and what they are going to do at every second."

Yahweh stopped and scratched the back of his head.

"The truth is, I don't stop it for the same reason no other god stops bad things from happening. We don't have the power to. We can do incredible things, but we can't force someone to do something they don't want to do, or vice versa. We can't stop the tide or halt the weather. These things are beyond our control, and those who can do such things are too large and powerful to care about what happens to basic life forms. They don't even care about us as gods; we don't even compare to them in scale or power."

"Like the Salanis?"

"Exactly like her. That said, she has taken quite the interest in this planet; but that's not important for now. I need to get going."

Father Brown nodded. "Nobody will ever believe this."

"Then you'll have to believe it for yourself."

Yahweh rose, walked to the door and gripped the handle. Father Brown tried to help but found he couldn't approach him. Yahweh opened the door and disappeared into the cold night.

Chapter 14

The archangels were dead. Michael could feel it in the very fibre of his being. His army, defeated by monsters, was in retreat, the angels fleeing for their lives. Enraged and looking to take his frustrations out on someone, he was elated when came across Ares while in flight.

The God of War seemed to share Michael's emotion, a scowl visible behind his Spartan helm. Michael pulled his angel blade from the holding space in his chest, the blue glow illuminating the night around him.

"This is where it ends for you," Michael said. "The Olympians lose their greatest fighter and will soon be dominated."

Ares coughed in amusement. "You must be as blind as you are stupid. Your army is done; your brothers and sisters are dead. You've lost the war."

"While I live, the war continues," Michael spat.

"What happened to you?" Ares asked. "When we first met all those years ago, you were calm and collected. I'd have expected this sort of ego trip from Raphael, not from you."

"Do not presume to know me," Michael said, sneering. "I did what I had to, to please my father. You were a job, nothing more."

"Where does this hostility come from? You can't tell me you've always hated us."

"Not always. Only since father began to favour you over us. We knew he'd favour the humans first, but I never would have thought you lot would have been his second choice."

"So, you're jealous that your daddy didn't love you as much as he used to?" Ares asked in shock. "Tell me, what have you done to deserve his love? What have you done to prove yourself worthy? Nothing! You lounge around in Heaven like some trust fund brat who thinks the world owes him everything. You know how I know? I was the same way. All of us were the same way. But we learned.

"Now, I'll give you an option. You can call off your battle and live peacefully with us. Create an alliance between the Asgardians, Olympians and Egyptians. "

Michael thought about it. Ares hadn't been wrong in stating the war was done. He had lost.. His best bet would be to take Ares's advice, start an alliance and maybe a whole new pantheon. It wasn't a difficult concept for him to wrap his head around. There would have to be negotiations and the like, but it was doable.

A surge of power in the north part of Red City hit him. He knew that power, the feel of energy flowing through him. His father had revealed himself. A plan crossed Michael's mind as his face twisted into a malicious grin.

"I appreciate your offer, Ares. You've been quite accommodating. I was so close to taking you up on it. But there's been a change of plans, and I'm afraid I have to decline."

Ares sighed, and the sorrow in his exhalation confused Michael. Ares was a war god; he thought Ares would have been giddy for the chance to kill the final archangel, or at the very least try.

"Let that be your folly," Ares grumbled, leaping at the archangel.

Michael struck at Ares, his angel blade deflecting off Ares's shield. The war god landed,, spun in place and leapt again. Pain greeted Michael as Ares's sword grazed the flesh of his lower leg; he hadn't thought he'd swing so low.

"Do you think this will work out well for you?" Michael asked.

"Come down here and fight!" Ares shouted. "Don't be a

coward."

"I am going to put you down from up here, just as I did with Athena."

Michael, who had done some reading of Olympian history, knew that Ares and Athena never really got along. They were both gods of combat, but they represented two different aspects of war. Athena was a tactician while Ares was chaos in the field of battle. He'd imagined Ares would have celebrated the death of his sister.

It came as a shock when Ares howled in anger and slashed once again at the archangel. The blade cut into Michael's chest, sending globules of glowing blood flying into the night. Michael didn't have time to fight Ares; he had to go to his father before He chose to conceal himself once again.

He threw his angel blade at Ares. While he raised his shield to block the attack, Michael flew away toward the source of the power. He surveyed the city below; monsters of mythic proportions roamed the streets, attacking whatever angels they could get their fangs and claws into. In the distance the power acted as a beacon, calling Michael to come closer.

The church was smaller than most, only big enough to seat perhaps fifty people. Michael scoffed at the disrespect of using such a small building to worship someone of his father's stature. Yahweh deserved mega-churches and hordes of holy men at his beck and call. A small building with only a single priest was an insult to the majesty of his father.

He swooped down to the ground, an act he felt beneath him; but if his father was willing to walk the earth, so would he, at least to greet him. The doors opened and Yahweh exited the church. Michael gazed upon his father; age had begun to set in earlier than it should have. His typically dark beard had gone white, while lines around his eyes showed prominently with every movement.

"Father," Michael said. "You're back."

'I am, Michael," God said, his voice low with disappointment.

"Why are you back? Why did you leave?"

"These are questions you have no right or place to ask, my

son," Yahweh chided. "Look at what you've done. The devastation you've brought to your home, the pain and suffering you've spawned. You've given power back to those who would have been happy never to have it again. You betrayed my wishes and broken the treaties I put in place so long ago.

"Even if you do win this war, and your odds are dwindling down to zero rapidly, the other pantheons will not take your actions lying down. You may have North America and most of Europe under your rule, but what happens when the Asian and African gods come to attack you? The Hindi gods will destroy you long before the Japanese gods even think to arrive.

"Michael, I credited you with so much more, but it seems I was wrong. I did know what you'd do, but I did what I had to do. I don't care that you tried to fill my shoes as the patron of Heaven. I encourage and applaud that sort of initiative. But you waged a war you couldn't win. You messed up, Michael, and I am not impressed."

Michael bowed his head while his father lectured him and told him how short-sighted his plan had been. Yahweh had spent centuries carving out a deal with the Asian and African gods, doing everything he could to ensure none of them came after his pantheon. The African gods allowed Egypt to be removed to make room for more of their own, not that it made much of a difference.

The Asian gods had been a little more difficult to deal with. They had wanted so much land as a major buffer zone between Yahweh's pantheon and their own. Michael had believed the African and Asian gods would have left the archangels alone in their fight. He had no quarrel with them, at least for the time being. He hadn't expected the fallen gods to put up as much of a fight as they had.

It would take some time to recreate archangels. Next time, he wouldn't make the same mistake of spreading everyone out. He would have them remain as a group, killing god after god. He would imbue them with the power and ability to kill gods naturally. Angel blades would no longer be necessary..

"Father," Michael said, interrupting, "will you forgive me for what I've done? Am I beyond redemption?"

Yahweh's features softened, as his eyes expressed sorrow and forgiveness.

"My child," he said, "nobody is beyond forgiveness if it is what they seek."

He reached out to Michael, indicating a desired embrace. Michael walked to his father and took him in his arms.

"I'm sorry for everything I've done," Michael whispered.

"I know you are, my son."

Michael's hand formed his angel blade and he slowly entered it into Yahweh's back. He could feel his father's body stiffen as he pulled himself away. Yahweh's eyes were wide, tears streaming down his face.

"It was always to end this way," he said, "As I have seen it."

Michael nodded in agreement. "So it shall always have been."

He pulled the angel blade from his father's back and ran it across Yahweh's throat. The god's eyes flashed with anger for a moment before going blank. His body faded and burst into millions of tiny lights. Michael puffed his chest out as the lights began to enter him, filling him with his father's power.

Ares had seen the whole ordeal. Michael had been mistaken if he thought such a cheap trick would stop the God of War. When Yahweh stepped out of the church and began shouting at Michael, Ares decided to stay out of sight and wait. He had no doubt the old god knew Ares was there watching, although he also doubted Yahweh would have given him anything to work with in defeating Michael.

He sighed through his nose, frustrated at how long the fight had taken. He'd had the chance to kill Michel, and Yahweh revealing himself had taken it away. He'd planned on whittling the angel's health down to the point where he couldn't possibly fight back.

Yahweh took Michael in for a hug, a nice touching moment until Michael stabbed his father in the back. Ares's eyes shot open in shock and alarm. He knew exactly what would happen next. He sent out a mental message to all the gods available; he'd need all the help he could get.

In a flash, Thor and Sekhmet were at his side.

"What's going —" Sekhmet began, but stopped as she saw Yahweh burst into lights.

Rage passed through Thor's eyes. He stood and rushed toward the archangel. He threw his small magic hammer Mjolnir, grinning as it connected with the archangel's face. A sickening crunch echoed through the street as Michael was sent flying backward.

The hammer returned to Thor's hand as Michael's face reset itself. The archangel stood and glared at Thor.

"I should have known you'd be here. Ares and Sekhmet can come out too. I can feel you; your presence is revealed to me."

Ares and Sekhmet did as they were bid, their surprise attack compromised. Ares placed his sword at his side and pulled out his spear. Sekhmet morphed into her lioness form, claws sprouting from her fingertips while fangs took shape in her elongating jaws. She emitted a low, guttural growl as she moved into pouncing position.

Thor joined Ares and Sekhmet.

"What's the plan?" Thor asked.

"I don't have one," Ares admitted. "That was Athena's competence. The best I have is to hit him until he dies."

"That's one strategy," Sekhmet said.

"Hit him until he dies?' Thor asked.

Ares shook his head, "Best I got so far."

Ares, shield up and spear out, ran toward the archangel. Michael didn't move or seem to care when Ares pushed the point of the spear through his chest. Michael looked down at his wound, light pouring from his body as he grabbed the shaft. He snapped the spear In two and pushed Ares backward.

Ares watched as Michael gripped the end of the spear still in his chest. He pulled the blade out and threw it to the ground, the hole in his chest healing almost instantly. Sekhmet attacked, sinking her claws into Michael's shoulders. While she kept the archangel busy, Thor rushed in and took Michael out at the legs.

Ares pulled the sword from his sheath and readied his next

attack. He watched Michael take the hits from Sekhmet and Thor without any attempt to fight back. Something seemed off, though Ares couldn't place it. He lifted his shield and ran at the archangel.

Michael drew his angel blade, striking the Olympian's shield, knocking Ares back several paces. Ares lifted an eyebrow, curious. He'd taken hits from all three without flinching, though he'd blocked the latest attack.

Something was strange, here; he just couldn't seem to grasp it. He wished Athena were in the fight with him; she would have figured out a way to take Michael down for good. He shook the thought from his head; Athena was dead and gone, no changing that. He had to figure things out for himself. Why did Michael retaliate when Ares attacked?

Michael got a grip on Sekhmet and threw her to the side. She landed perfectly on her feet; her claws dug into the ground to anchor herself. Thor continued to fight Michael, keeping the archangel busy.

"Hang on a second," Ares said. "I think I might have figured something out. We need to keep attacking him."

"So what we're doing?"

"Sort of, but not really," Ares said, "Hang back and message to the others, we need a distraction."

Sekhmet nodded and stepped back as Ares rushed Michael. The archangel saw him coming, but did nothing to stop the Olympian from attacking. Ares's sword sliced through Michael's body, separating the top half from the bottom. Ares pushed the top half with his shield and waited. Thor took the opportunity to smash the archangel's head with his hammer.

The gods stepped away waiting for confirmation that Michael had truly died. The light blood spread from both halves of the archangel's body, meeting in the middle. The blood began to glow a deep blue, then turned red and back to white. The light became blinding as Michael's body brought itself together and repaired the damage.

Michael's head grew back, revealing a wide grin.

"You're all just so adorable with how much you're trying," Michael taunted. "You can't kill me."

Ares smirked, the last puzzle piece falling into place in his head. Psychically, Ares relayed his plan to each of the gods and goddesses he could reach.

"Individually, no we can't. As a group, though," Ares paused for dramatic effect "As a group, we will kill you."

Sekhmet looked at Ares. "Let's do this."

"For the honour and glory of the elder gods!" Thor bellowed.

As the three gods attacked together, Michael's face contorted into a mixture of fear and determination. The angel blade appeared once again, deflecting Ares's attack while Sekhmet and Thor landed their hits. But Michael didn't budge under the weight of Thor's hammer; whatever was going on, he was getting stronger.

"Hit him with everything you got!" Ares shouted.

Sekhmet's claws sank into Michael's back in a place where he couldn't reach her. She bit down into the base of his wings, successfully removing one while the other beat frantically to bat her away. Thor attacked again, hitting Michael in the chest with his hammer. Mjolnir bounced off Michael's chest, resulting in the archangel's laughter.

"What else do you have to offer Thor?"

Ares missed his thrust and flew to the side onto his shield. Thor caught the back of Michael's hand and was sent crashing against the walls of the church. Michael managed to grab Sekhmet's tail and flung her, spinning, several meters away.

"Okay," Michael sneered, "I'm getting real sick of this. I'm just going to kill you all and get on with my night."

"You think you can?" Ares asked, eyebrow raised. "I know your weakness."

"Oh, do you," Michael snorted.

"You have to be hit by all three of us at the same time. It took me a while to figure it out, but here we are. Well, not us three specifically, but by an Egyptian, Olympian and Asgardian."

"Do you think you can manage that?"

"With just the three of us? No. But they can."

Ares looked up to see gods and goddesses appear around them. Each deity held a projectile weapon in their hands.

"Tell me," Ares said, climbing to his feet, "what do you think the odds are that three arrows from different pantheons will strike you?"

Michael's face showed fear, but he soon rearranged his features to display a cool arrogance.

"Zero percent," he said. "Not a single arrow will hit me. You really think that such a cheap tactic would amount to anything?"

"It's worth a shot."

At the word shot, the gods unleashed the arrows from their bows. . Michael's angel blade slashed at the arrows as they passed harmlessly through the gods and Michael, revealing them to be nothing more than illusions.

While Michael was distracted the gods attacked as one. Ares's sword hit Michael in the lower back while Thor's hammer connected with the back of his head and Sekhmet's claws dug into the flesh of Michael's arm.

Time seemed to stop as the weapons made simultaneous contact. Michael screamed, sound waves emitted from his mouth as the volume rose to ear-splitting decibels. Glass shattered in the distance and power poles caught fire as the electricity coursed through the lines arced against the wood.

Ares, Sekhmet and Thor were sent flying backward as Thor's hammer removed Michael's head from his body. Pure light and energy surged from Michael's wounds. Ares shielded his eyes from the light as best he could. The light was stronger than he'd anticipated, piercing Ares's mind, leaving him blinded internally. He screamed as the heat began to cook his flesh and rend his soul asunder.

Ares opened his eyes to a white backdrop. "Where am I?" he asked.

"You're in the space between life and death. This is the white light everyone sees before they die," a voice said.

Ares spun to face Yahweh. "You!"

"Yeah."

"What's going on here?"

Yahweh sighed. "It's complicated."

"Doesn't look like I have anywhere else to be," Ares snarled. "Enlighten me."

"Very well." he agreed. "I was a bit of an angry god in my early days. I wanted all the power and couldn't let anyone else hold any domain. That said, I did some things I seriously regret. After a couple hundred years, I'd learned how wrong I was though. But, by that time I couldn't take it back, the deals had been made. I'm sorry for that."

"Is this going anywhere?" Ares asked, "Or is this just an apology?"

"Yes, just hold on a second," Yahweh snapped. "When I was at war with the Egyptians, they were royally kicking my ass. I managed to kill many of them, as well; their victor certainly would have been pyrrhic, but a victory none the less. So, I spoke with Michael and placed a few caveats on him. He could only be killed by members of three different pantheons, so when he died, he would kill everything around him, and his death would mark the end of everything."

"You're a monster," Ares said. "I can't believe you'd be such a sore loser that you'd go so far as to do such a thing."

Yahweh raised his hand in surrender.

"You're right. I was a maniac and a fool and reprehensible beyond any level of forgiveness. But I did what I did and there was no going back on it. The best I could do was try to dampen the reaction of Michael's death.

"I knew Michael would try to kill me. Had I fought him, it would have ended with both our deaths and the inevitable end of everything."

"So, what you did, those glowing lights you turned into," Ares said, "Those were to dampen what would happen?"

"Yes. I can't fully stop everything that's going to happen; that's why you're in the half-space. You being here will give you the power needed to stop what I've started, but, it will result in the deaths of every god except for two: Sif's child, as per Death's promise, and one other."

"Which one?" Ares asked.

"I don't know. I can't see that far ahead."

"Do you know when it's going to happen?"

"Tough to say. Maybe within the next fifty years, maybe as far out as a hundred years. For all I know, it could happen next year."

"Sort of makes all this fighting pointless."

"Does it?" Yahweh asked. "Maybe your initial reason for fighting was pointless, but it doesn't change the fact that you saved humanity from a would-be tyrant. That's nothing to be ashamed of or angry about. You all did a good thing, and I will honour all the dead gods in the only way I know how."

"What way is that?"

"By not forgetting them." Yahweh said, a glimmer in his eye. "I'm not dead, after all. I'm just trapped in the in-between. I am no longer able to interact with the underworld or the physical world. A suitable prison, I'd say."

"An eternity of loneliness," Ares replied. "I'm not sure even you deserve such a fate."

"Regardless," Yahweh said, "it's the fate I chose for myself. I knew what I was doing before I chose it and I do not in any way feel bad for myself. I regret what I've done, but I deserve my fate. I may spend my eternity alone, but once this universe finally dies, I will be able to die with it. It's just a matter of time and patience."

Ares bowed his head to the great god

"I commend your sacrifice then. You died with honour, and you shall spend the rest of your existence with honour. I will honour you by not forgetting you. I will also tell others that you live, that you took only a small part of this war and the part you played was to the benefit of the mortals."

"It is appreciated," Yahweh said.

"Why are you talking to me, and not any of the others?"

"I am talking with the others," Yahweh said. "Physics and time here are . . . odd. They work in a way that makes very little sense. Basically, I'm able to have several one-on-one conversations at the same time while retaining all the information and maintaining focus as if only one conversation is taking place at any given time."

"You're right, this place is odd. It's almost as if this place makes absolutely no sense whatsoever. Like it doesn't have any of the rules the physical world is held to. There's not time, space or anything here. It's nothing, but everything. I don't understand this place, and I doubt you do either."

"I'll have a long time to get it figured out."

Ares shrugged in acceptance and looked around. "So, how do I get out of here?"

"Do you want to leave?" Yahweh asked. "If you stay here, you'll be safe from the coming deity purge and can live your life —"

"In a world of pure abstract that makes absolutely no sense until the end of all eternity?" Ares interrupted, "No, I think I'm good. I have to get back to the physical world. Or, you can just let me die and that will be that. Frankly, which direction I go is up to you."

"You're kind of a moody prick, you know that?" Yahweh said.

"I've been accused of it a time or two," Ares said.

"I like you, Ares," Yahweh said. "I'll send you back to the world of the living. I know I can't interact with the outside world, but I hope you're the one who survives the purge."

Ares raised his chin as a sign of strength. "I guess only time will tell."

"Indeed."

Ares stepped to the side, and a white light enveloped him. It did not carry the same heat of Michael's explosion, but brought a friendly warmth. He felt his body rise and was soon greeted by the cold air of the Red City night. He coughed and looked down at his hand. He was all right.

Sekhmet coughed beside him, "Did you see him too?' she asked, her body shifting back to her human form.

"I did," Ares said, "I don't know what to think of all that."

Thor grabbed his hammer and walked to them. "Where's the body?" he asked.

"I don't think there is one," Sekhmet replied.

"Well," Ares said, the memory of Yahweh locked in his head. "I guess we won."

Chapter 15

The gods convened at the same meeting hall in which they'd held their Gathering only days before. Zeus and Odin stood on the stage, their faces mournful at the loss of Ra. The Egyptians stood in the corner of the room, close to the stage.

Odin stepped forward to speak.

"We've won the war, but at a great cost. We've lost many fellow gods, many of whom were near and dear to our hearts."

Sif sat alone with her child. Memories of Apollo shifted through her mind, including the final mental image of him getting an angel blade to the head. Painfully, she raised her head and brought her attention back to the stage.

"Unfortunately, although the war is over, we will continue to suffer losses. Zeus and I have to go away. It's not something either of us wants to do, but because of the deals we made to win the war, we must. A deal with a god is unbreakable, for all parties.

"I will ask you to talk amongst yourselves to choose a new leader for each pantheon. This will not be an easy decision, as there are many of you, and a pantheon is a thing of massive proportions. The leader will have to be in charge not only of the gods and mortals, but of the full creation of your new home."

Thoth stood to the side, scratching every word in his notebook as they were spoken.

"Why do we need to split things into three?" Sif asked. "Why not just have one large pantheon, as before?"

All the deities turned to look at her.

"All together?" Thor asked.

"Yes," Sif said, "Ra had mentioned combining the pantheons together. At the time, I think it was for survival, but now? Now it could be to help build the world and create a place beyond compare."

"Some of us may have to change what we are the gods of," Bastet chimed in. "Otherwise, there's bound to be some overlap. Thor, do you still want to be God of Thunder?"

"Maybe not something quite so narrow. Maybe a god of weather?"

"Thoth, I'm sure you still want to be a god of scribes?"

Thoth nodded, still writing.

"Yes, I shall continue to be a muse to the authors and record keepers."

"What about you?" Bastet asked Sif. "What do you want to be goddess of?"

Sif's face flushed.

"I don't really know. Maybe motherhood? I was the first goddess among us to give birth."

The gods nodded, glancing fondly at the child in her hands. Many of the goddesses had been visibly jealous of her child, though with the restrictions lifted and their new found godhood, the goddesses could finally reproduce once again.

"Still," Odin said, "that still leaves the question of who will lead you."

Hades stood. "I will lead them."

"You?" Odin asked.

"Why not?"

"No reason," Odin said. "You're certainly qualified. I just thought you'd rather go back to the underworld."

Hades shook his head.

"The underworld has been in good shape since I've left. Though my home used to be there, I can't help but feel I'd be encroaching on Lucifer's territory. So, if nobody objects, I will lead the gods to their new pantheon."

Odin looked to the crowd, their faces blank.

"Any objections?" Odin asked, but the crowd remained silent. "Anybody else want to throw their hat in to the running for leader?"

Once again, nobody said a word. In an instant, Hades had been named the new ruler of the elder gods.

"Thank you," Hades said, his face stoic. "As your new leader, there will some changes to how we do things. I don't want to change too much too quickly, but I do have a few things to say.

"First of all, I want to grant Lucifer deity status; he will no longer be an archangel. I make this decision based on the help he gave during our war. He was instrumental in our victory and such actions should not go unrewarded. He will become a member of our pantheon and we shall grant him use of the resources we produce in the future.

"My second decree is that we will not aid or be a part of humanity until we get our pantheon up and running. They are a capable lot who seem to have done well for themselves in the past fifty years without any gods guiding them.

"Finally, my third decree will be that no two gods may carry the same platform. There are a number of us and that may be difficult; ,but, we have all spent our time on Earth learning new skills. We should be able to take on new deity roles."

The gods stood silent, unsure of what to say about Hades' decrees. They didn't disagree with anything he'd said, though they could have used some rest before they had to start deciding on deific roles.

"When do we start?" Thoth asked. "Just so I can start jotting things in my book to make them official."

"We will begin constructing the pantheon in a year's time. While we wait, we will rest, choose our platforms, and build from there. We will continue to live among the humans, many of whom still would not know our faces. We will be safe and secure within our homes until such a time as we begin building."

Set raised his hand.

"What do we call ourselves? I'm sure as shit not going to be known as an Olympian or an Asgardian."

"We won't be known as any of those. We will be known as Elder Gods from now on. Yes, it does make us sound old, but in all fairness, we are. We are not long for this world. I believe we will have another thousand years or so until most us begin to die of old age. That's just the way things are."

The gods looked at each other, unsure how to react to the knowledge they would die sooner than they'd like; but they accepted the explanation Hades gave and chose not to press the issue.

"One last thing before you are all excused," Hades said. "I would like to thank Zeus and Odin personally for their sacrifices. They may not have fallen in battle, but they chose to give their lives for our victory, even if the deaths were to be delayed until afterward. We could not have won without the choices they'd made. So, on behalf of the Elder Gods, I thank you both for everything you've done. I would also like to thank you both for being excellent rulers of the past regime and would like to say that living up to the example you both set will not be easy."

Zeus grinned and placed his hand on Hades' shoulder. "You will do fine my brother."

Zeus and Odin turned and bowed to the gods and, in a flash, they were gone.

Hades returned his gaze to the others.

"Things are not going to be the same for us; Michael and his angels made sure of that. We all lost those we loved and unfortunately, there's no bringing them back. We must remain strong. We must not allow their deaths to be in vain.

"So now I ask you, my fellow deities, to go live your lives for the next year. Rest and become the gods you need to be. Thoth will be visiting everyone and taking down the necessary information. We will build our pantheon, and once it is completed, we will reveal ourselves to humanity. We will be their gods and they will worship us as before. With their worship, we will aid them through their lives and help them become the best humanity could be. We will create a utopia on Earth. You all have my promise."

A grand gesture for humanity: Sif loved the sentiment, although she couldn't believe such a utopia could ever exist alongside humanity. Their nature wouldn't allow it. Instead of voicing her opinion, she remained silent, allowing the gods to burst into a thunderous roar of approval and joy.

Thoth peered at her and nodded. He wrote in his book as she felt her platform become motherhood. She breathed a sigh of relief and tended to her child.

Lucifer sat on his throne. He'd felt Hades give him true deity status, a gift he wished he could have returned with a kind thank you card and a letter explaining why he didn't want to be a god. Such things were not within his grasp, though; instead, he looked out over the vast underworld before him. From his throne, he could see the three afterlives and those within.

A jet of fire shot from his nose as he sighed..

"Beelzebub, do you think we'll be all right now?" he asked his right-hand demon.

"I can't say. Things will be different, although I imagine you'll be left to your own devices as per usual."

Lucifer nodded, resting his chin in his hand.

"I suppose. I mean, I enjoy the solitude, and of all the high demons, you're certainly the best to have a conversation with."

"Your words mean a lot to me, my lord."

"Although, you are compelled to worship me in that way. You have no idea how much I want someone to talk to that doesn't have to kiss my ass at any given moment. To actually have someone to challenge my authority."

"Abaddon did that before," Beelzebub mentioned.

"Yes, you're right, but it's not the same. He wanted to overthrow me. He was my Michael, and just like Michael, unsuccessful. Although, I did keep him alive."

"If you call that living," Beelzebub muttered.

Lucifer ignored the remark from the high demon and continued to mope.

"Oh, and you know what else those assholes I helped are doing? They're dumping all their pets on me. 'Don't worry, they can help you,' they said. 'We made a deal that says they can eat souls.' Where do they get off?"

"May I speak frankly?" Beelzebub asked.

"Of course," Lucifer said. "I encourage it, not that it'll last with you."

Beelzebub nodded in agreement with the accusation.

"There is a plus side to this monster thing. Actually, there are a few advantages."

"Do tell."

"Well, you can have a companion. The monsters are not compelled to agree with everything you say. Some of them can talk and may be able to give you the conversations you so desire."

The tips of Lucifer's mouth curled into the start of a smile. He tapped the end of his chin.

"What else?"

"Well," Beelzebub continued, "they could finally clear out The Pit. It's getting really deep. How long did it take you to get down there last time?"

"Point taken," Lucifer said. "It is getting pretty bad down there, and it's not like they're ever going to be anywhere else. I may as well give their souls rest and allow them a mercy killing."

"Along with that, they could bring on a whole new dynamic to punishments. Imagine the killers being annihilated by a chimera, or souls being speared by a manticore?"

"All right, I'll accept the monsters. I'm sure Ammit wouldn't mind a few souls here and there."

"That's the way to think about it," Beelzebub said.

Lucifer thought for a moment.

"Gather Mephistopheles and Baal. We need to talk about the future of the underworld and what my newly appointed godhood will mean for all of us."

Beelzebub bowed and vanished. Lucifer stood and gazed out his window, thinking. He could change the fabric of reality in the underworld with his power. He could mix the good with the bad, force the mediocre to strive for something greater, introduce reincarnation. The options were almost boundless. Yet he couldn't help but feel as if he shouldn't do as his ambitions desired.

While he waited for his high demons to arrive, he considered their roles in his new underworld. They were necessary before, each overlooking one of the three underworlds: Baal resided over Paradise, Mephistopheles over The Fields and Beelzebub over Hell. With his new power, he could reside over all three without the help of the others. He didn't want to force them out of their jobs, but he worried over the possibility of boredom from allowing them to continue with their jobs, or the inevitable uprising if he forced them out to become bystanders.

He had an idea though. It was not the best idea he'd ever had, but the sort that could work well with the right circumstance.

The high demons appeared before him.

"You summoned us, my master," Mephistopheles said with a bow.

"I did," Lucifer said. "And don't bow. I hate that."

"Very well," Mephistopheles said.

"What do you wish of us?' Baal asked.

Lucifer sat back in his throne and grinned.

"I'm sending the three of you to Earth with your demons."

"What?" Baal asked. "Is that allowed?"

"I don't care if it is or not, I'm doing it anyway. It's not like they're going to do anything about it.. They can't rescind my deity status."

"Why are you sending us up there, though?" Mephistopheles asked.

"I want you to join the Supernatural Council. You're going to take all the demons and live amongst the humans under the rule of the supernatural council."

"Really?" Baal asked. "Why?"

"Three reasons. One, because I don't need you down here anymore. I can do everything here myself. Two, because I want to be able to keep an eye on the angels. Their archangels are gone, and they'll be frantic. You joining the supernatural council will bring them on to join and as such will give them purpose and allow me to watch them. And three, because it's going to be the best place for you and all the demons. You'll be able to live freely and do as you wish, provided it doesn't infringe on their laws. I'll expect you all to be on your best behaviour. After all, you're representing the underworld, and I don't want them thinking we're a bunch of hacks down here."

The high demons looked at each other in wonderment.

"Who will be the member on the council?" Beelzebub asked. "You can't leave it to us. We'll fight over it."

It was true; the demons would likely kill each other for the role of leader.

"Mephistopheles will be on the council," Lucifer said. "Baal and Beelzebub will be your right and left hands. They will ensure the demons are doing everything properly."

"I think they have hunters for that," Baal said.

"Indeed, they do, including hunters who kill demons. But, with the might of you three, you will ensure that no demon comes under the blade of a hunter. If a demon becomes unruly, you will do it yourself."

The high demons bowed.

"As you command," they said in unison.

The demons vanished, leaving Lucifer alone once again. It would be a few days before the monsters would arrive in the underworld, and until that time, Lucifer decided, he would take up reading. It had been a good long while since he'd read a good book.

Zeus stood atop Olympus. The mountain no longer shook when he set foot upon the stones. He had the power needed to kill Typhon and save him from a terrible fate. Though, the vow he'd made would ultimately kill him, breaking the oath would end him in a more horrific way than Typhon could have ever dreamed of inflicting.

Odin was trapped in the underworld, bound by the same chain once used to bind Fenrir. Zeus wanted to save him, but the vow had been made and he had to be present to watch the great wolf devour human souls, two each year. Zeus didn't know how long it would take to eat a soul, though he didn't doubt the wolf would prolong the pain and suffering for as long as possible.

He looked up at the sky, then out to Greece. He'd loved his land, the place he'd once called home. He couldn't get back into the castle in Olympus; the place had been closed and likely was destroyed by angels a millennium ago.

He sighed, preparing himself for what must happen.

"I, Zeus, call upon the creature Typhon!"

As before, the ground shook and the sky darkened. In a matter of seconds, Typhon descended from the sky. A smirk formed on the monster's face.

"I didn't expect you to live up to your end of the bargain. You're a god, fully formed now; you could have broken the oath."

Zeus couldn't have broken the bond if he'd been the being that created the universe. As a lowly Earth god, he'd have stood no chance at all. Typhon had tested him.

"My word is my bond," Zeus said. "I live by it and soon enough, I will die by it."

"Your bravery is commendable, King of Olympus."

"Not king anymore."

"I suppose that is true."

"Look," Zeus said, "I don't have all day. If you're going to do this, then do it. Otherwise, release me from the bond and I can go my way."

"I'd wanted to be nice. Give you a chance to come up with some meaningful last words. But, if you're in such a hurry..."

Typhon opened his mouth; several rows of long jagged teeth lined his gums. Typhon's breath was hot, burning the clothes from Zeus's skin. The King of Olympians remained unaffected by the fiery breath and walked forward climbing into Typhon's mouth. Typhon closed his jaw and swallowed, sending Zeus down the creature's esophagus.

"I should let you know," Typhon said, "now that I'm free; Greece is going to burn, as will the rest of the Mediterranean. Any place that once worshiped you, will burn."

Zeus grinned; he'd planned on letting the creature live. With the new revelation, he was permitted to not hold back. His end of the bargain had been fulfilled. He charged himself, preparing to release enough electricity to kill the monster.

Zeus exploded the moment he touched Typhon's stomach acid, sending more electricity than he'd ever released. Zeus's body became no more as the current travelled along Typhon's body.

The screech from Typhon could be heard through Greece, Zeus was sure of it, though none would know the cause. Cells began to break down in Typhon's body, disintegrating the creature bit by bit. In minutes, both Zeus and Typhon were no more.

It pained Ares to leave his kin and comrades. He looked at the gathering hall, feeling the presence of everyone inside.

"Are you just going to stand there?" Athena asked.

Ares glanced to the construct of his mind. Since the death of Michael and his emergence from the In-Between, Athena had been there with him. He knew she wasn't a ghost or a spectral form; she was nothing more than his own mind playing tricks on him.

"Yeah," Ares said. "I'm just going to stand here. If I go in, I'll be talked into staying, and I just can't do it. I can't be a god anymore."

"But you are one," Athena said. "There's nothing you can do about it."

He regarded his sister, dressed in her favourite red leather jacket. She wore a white shirt and blue jeans. Her face wore no makeup; her godly beauty didn't require any.

"I am a god," Ares agreed, "but that doesn't mean I have to agree to act like one. I can hear them in there, talking about who they want to be, their future pantheon and what they plan to do with humanity. It's just all so pointless. It's just posturing, plain and simple. I can't be a part of it."

"You're not wrong."

"There are just so many more pressing concerns to deal with."

"The end of everything? Just as Yahweh told you?"

Ares nodded. "I can't allow it to happen. I don't know how I'm going to stop it, or even if I can. But I can at least try."

Athena scratched her nose. Her movements were so real; it was difficult for Ares to accept she was just a mental image.

"You'd best get going on it. Who knows how long you have, or even what's going to happen?"

"I'm sure I can figure it out."

"I can't imagine how. You've never been considered a particularly bright deity."

"That may be so," Ares said, "but in some myths you're considered a bitch."

Ares turned away from the gathering hall and began to walk down the road. The gods wouldn't likely be leaving by the front door, though he didn't want to take the chance. The open road was a welcome change from his usual scenery. He didn't dare teleport; the last thing he wanted was to have the gods find him using his powers.

"In all seriousness though," Athena said, "We really should try and figure this out. We may not have a lot of time."

"I know, and that scares the ever-loving shit out of me."

"Although," Athena said, "a thought does occur."

Ares raised an eyebrow. "This should be good."

"Yahweh was an earthbound deity; he shouldn't have had the power or ability to end everything."

"I thought the same thing," Ares said. "But being an earthbound deity only means he can manipulate things on Earth. That doesn't mean he didn't go travelling the cosmos for a time. He could have made some friends or stumbled upon a power he didn't fully understand. He wasn't exactly a popular deity in his early days. It's not a stretch to think that he could have spent some time away from Earth until he found a contingency plan, just in case he lost his wars."

"You're smarter than I gave you credit for."

Ares stopped walking

"Athena, I know you're a figment in my mind. You're a projection caused by something I don't even know. But I think this is as good a time as any to say something I've wanted to say for a while."

"What's up?" Athena asked.

"Look, I was a shit brother for a very long time," Ares said with a deep sigh. "I never really said this, but I'm sorry. I'm sorry for making your life hard, I'm sorry for being that brash, dumb dickhead that just made things worse. I was jealous of how much Father loved you, I was jealous of your brain and I wanted nothing more than to see you lose everything. I just want to say I'm sorry for who I used to be."

"Do you think maybe that's why you're seeing me?" she asked. "As a personal punishment?"

"If that were the case, there should be a lot more people following me around. No, I think you're here for a reason. I just don't know what it is yet."

"Should be fun figuring it out," Athena said, her smile softening him.

Ares nodded, and recommenced walking down the road.

"Know any good songs?"

"Songs?"

"We're probably going to be walking down this road a while. It might pass the time if we sing a bit."

Athena nodded. "Ever hear Elemental Weapon?"

Ares let out a loud belly laugh. "It's been a while, but I think I know what song you're thinking of."

"Apt, considering what we've been through."

Athena cleared her throat and began to sing the first few lines of *From Asgard to Olympus*, a song about the band's members going to both pantheons and murdering the gods. Ares grinned, carrying on the tune as he walked down the road.

In the distance he could hear a car approaching. Ares turned and stuck out his thumb.

Acknowledgments

This book was for the most part a solo effort. Not a lot of people went into the creation of this novel, so I'm afraid this bit might be a little short.

I would like to thank my editor Joanne Paulson for her excellent job. This book is a thousand times better than what it was because of her editing as well as the notes she sent along with the manuscript.

I would like to thank Alexi Beauchemin for being the first (and only) person to read this story as it was originally written, as a graphic novel script. Her excitement for the story let me know that I'd finally done a good job.

I would like to thank my ex-girlfriend for losing the original graphic novel script, forcing me to write it as a novel.

I would like to than my sister and Mum for giving me advice and ultimately helping me create my cover.

And most of all, I'd like to thank my parents and siblings for their consistent love and support while I chase my dream. I seriously couldn't do it without you guys.

Thank you all so much!

Author's Note

Thank you for taking the time to read my book. I hope you enjoyed it. If you did, please consider rating and reviewing on Amazon and Goodreads. I know it seems like a hassle, but to an Indie author like me, it means everything.

About the Author

Quinn Wayne Buckland was born in Fairview, Alberta, Canada, and has lived all over the province. The eldest of three siblings, his love of writing was apparent from age 12 when he started writing too many short stories to count, as well as songs and poems.

Quinn spends his time absorbing what can only be described as an unhealthy amount of science fiction media. That, of course is when he's not writing or playing with his lovely dog, Pepper.
He is a devout Atheist.

Made in the USA
Columbia, SC
02 June 2019